"I'm sober, P—— girls. And yo——

At first, his voic—— —— blanket, deep and smooth. Then reality kicked in and she snapped back. "You don't have the right to see the girls or me. You haven't been around for eight years."

"I know I don't deserve a second chance, but God has changed my life...."

She hated the thrill that warred with the fury at seeing him. He looked good. Older. A little more worn, but still so handsome he made her heart beat faster.

She spat the words through gritted teeth. "You need to leave. You have no right…"

He lifted his hands in surrender. "I'm not going to say anything to them. I never planned to without your permission." He placed his hands against his chest. "But I want to see them. Just see what they look like. That's all."

He could never get those years back with Pamela and with his girls, but he planned to spend the rest of his life making it up to them.

Books by Jennifer Johnson

Love Inspired Heartsong Presents

A Heart Healed
A Family Reunited

JENNIFER JOHNSON

and her unbelievably supportive husband, Albert, are happily married and raising three daughters: Brooke, Hayley and Allie. Besides being a middle-school teacher, Jennifer loves to read, write and chauffeur her girls. She is a member of American Christian Fiction Writers. Blessed beyond measure, Jennifer hopes to always think like a child—bigger than imaginable and with complete faith.

JENNIFER JOHNSON

A Family Reunited

HEARTSONG

PRESENTS

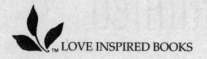

™ LOVE INSPIRED BOOKS

ISBN-13: 978-0-373-48678-6

A FAMILY REUNITED

Copyright © 2013 by Jennifer Johnson

www.Harlequin.com

Printed in U.S.A.

But with you there is forgiveness, so that we can,
with reverence, serve you.
—*Psalms* 130:4

This book is dedicated to my mother-in-law, Joyce Sallee. Despite overwhelming obstacles, you raised a son who loves the Lord. Like Jack and Pamela in the story, Al and I married and started a family very young, but by the Lord's grace and your guidance, Al became a man I respect and love. I will always thank God for you!

Chapter 1

"We're pregnant!"

Pamela Isaacs's jaw dropped as she looked up at her older brother, Kirk, and his wife, Callie. Squeals and cackles erupted as Pamela's daughters, parents and younger brother enveloped the expectant couple in hugs. They deserved a baby. Callie had fought and defeated breast cancer two years ago. Pamela knew they'd yearned for a child, and yet jealousy tickled her heart.

Pushing away her selfishness, she smiled and enfolded her sister-in-law in an embrace. "I'm so happy for you."

"Thanks. I couldn't believe it. When I went for the checkup, I never dreamed…"

Pamela grabbed both of Callie's hands in hers. "You'd receive the perfect surprise."

Callie nodded as the family headed into the living

area and settled into seats. Pamela's mother, Tammie, clasped her hands and lifted her gaze to the ceiling. "God is so good!"

Pamela forced herself not to roll her eyes. If she heard one more word about the awesomeness of God, she was going to hurl. It wasn't that she didn't believe in Him. Having been raised in a Christian home and having worked with creation on the family farm, she didn't deny His existence. But life had taught her not to trust Him when things got rough.

"When are you due?"

"How'd you find out?"

Questions flitted from each of the family members, and Pamela watched as her eight- and nine-year-old daughters dropped to the floor, one on each side of Callie's legs. Their faces shone with delight and eagerness to hear about their new cousin. Emma and Emmy had never had the opportunity to be around relatives their own age, even though their father had siblings who were only a few years older than the girls.

Jack. Just thinking his name made her blood burn through her veins. Her so-called husband had been gone eight years. Eight. Over the past year, he'd called and hung up on her many times over; then today he'd called asking to see their daughters.

He had no right to see the girls.

"Twins!" Her dad, Mike's, voice boomed through the room.

Pamela blinked away her thoughts and stared at Kirk and Callie. Kirk waved a sonogram through the air. His eyes lit up like a Christmas tree, though October was too early to turn on twinkling lights.

"You're having twins?" Emma exclaimed.

Pamela studied her older daughter. With long red hair pulled back in a ponytail, she looked so much like Pamela had at that age. Around her ears and the nape of her neck corkscrew curls escaped the band. Taller than most of her peers, she sported a gangly physique and a lot of freckles. Her crystal-blue eyes shimmered with delight.

Callie nodded. "We are." She tapped Emma's nose and then Emmy's. "One baby for each of you to hold."

Emmy jumped off the floor and yelled, "Woo hoo!"

Emmy was only a year younger than Emma and so close in appearance, except that Emmy sported deep dimples in each cheek when she smiled. The girls could almost be confused for twins except that Emma had had a recent growth spurt and now stood a full head taller than her younger sister.

"I can't believe it." Mom grabbed the sonogram from Kirk's hand, and she and Dad looked at the picture. She waved her free hand in front of her face as her deep green eyes glistened with tears.

"With all the noise and smells those two will produce, I reckon I'll have to stay in Knoxville." Ben chuckled. Her younger brother was in his last year of school at the University of Tennessee.

"No way." Kirk elbowed him. "Your help is gonna be needed around here when the babies come. Somebody's gotta run the farm, the orchard, the play area and petting zoo. Mom and Dad and Pamela already take care of the gift shop, café and bed-and-breakfast."

Ben's features hardened. Pamela knew Kirk made the comment in jest, but it was obvious her little brother didn't want anything to do with working in the family's business. Not that she could blame him. She had two more years until she graduated from college. Only two. Then she would have her accounting degree and could hightail it out of Bloom Hollow, Tennessee. She could take the girls anywhere she wanted and rebuild their lives together.

Most likely she'd stay in Tennessee, would probably even find an apartment close by. But she'd be in her own place, not living in the small cabin behind her family's bed-and-breakfast that doubled as the main home. She wanted to make her own way. Be her own person. Not just a member of the Jacobs Family Farm.

Her dad and brothers became engrossed in conversation. She couldn't hear what they said, but it triggered a memory of Jack standing with Dad several years ago, discussing how to work out the farm schedule. Jack had promised to work certain hours, but inevitably several days a week something else came up. He always had a reason, and he never lied about where he was or what he was doing. The problem was that a drunken stupor was usually the reason he failed to do his job.

The phone conversation she'd had with Jack earlier that day traipsed through her mind.

"I'm sober, Pamela. I want to see the girls. And you."

At first his voice had covered her like a warm blanket, deep and smooth. She'd found herself wanting to see him. Then common sense kicked in, and she snapped back to reality. "You don't have the right to see the girls or me. You haven't been around for eight years."

"I know I don't deserve a second chance, but God has changed my life…."

She scowled at the memory. He'd found God. Why did everyone she knew think they could say God's name and suddenly all was right in the world? When Callie had shared about the loss of both of her parents to cancer and then had had to endure the disease herself, everyone had been so quick to chime in, "God is sovereign. He'll see her through." When Pamela's high school friend Greta had died in a car accident, the very same people had done the same song and dance.

If God was so sovereign, why did He allow the bad things to begin with? Why couldn't life be simpler for those who loved and followed Him? She'd been full of faith and love when she and Jack had married right out of high school ten years ago. She'd trusted God with everything. But then Jack had started drinking, and he'd left. And life was never the same.

Jack Isaacs shoved the $15,000 check in his front jeans pocket. Two years and ten months. That's how long he'd saved to send Pamela the check. How long he'd been sober. How long God had been in charge of his life.

He couldn't deny the hurt when Pamela had returned the letter and check a few months ago. And he'd fought uncertainty since their phone call earlier that day, when she'd emphatically rejected the idea of meeting with him. He hadn't expected her to run back into his arms, but he'd believed she'd at least accept the money.

A slow grin lifted his lips. It had been nice to hear her voice. Maybe when she saw him in person, she'd take the cash. Excitement swelled in his chest at the idea of seeing Pamela again. He'd worn out the wallet-size high school senior picture of her that he'd clutched while praying God would keep him from touching the bottle when temptation arose.

He looked around the small bedroom he'd called home for almost three years. Clean white walls. Firm twin-size bed. Small wooden desk and chair. Four-drawer dresser that was missing two handles. Everything he owned had been shoved into a beat-up suitcase that he'd already put in the trunk of his car and the cardboard box that still sat on the bed.

When he'd first come to God's Hands, he'd wanted only one thing: a place to sleep for the night. He'd drunk himself into a stupor and hadn't eaten a real meal in over a month; he'd just wanted somewhere warm to lay his head. The tent he'd been sleeping in on the outskirts of town had done its job well, but winter had rolled around and the weather had been unbearably cold at night. Somehow, that December night, he'd happened on this particular homeless shelter. And God had more than one night's sleep planned for Jack's life.

Blowing out a long breath, he lifted up the cardboard box, walked outside to the used economy car he'd purchased, placed his belongings in the trunk then headed back inside.

God's Hands had been his home the past three years, and though it seemed strange, he ached with the knowledge that in a few hours' time he would leave the shelter and the state of Texas for good. He might return on occasion to visit his parents, but they lived several hours away, so most likely today would be the last time he'd see the shelter.

Jermaine, the director, placed a dark, calloused hand on Jack's shoulder. "You gonna help serve breakfast for old times' sake?"

"Without a doubt."

Jack followed his mentor into the brick building. He'd miss the sixty-year-old man who'd led him to the Lord, sat with him as he fought through his addiction and helped him find a job and get back in college. He'd never be able to repay Jermaine for all he'd done in Jack's life. If asked, Jack knew what Jermaine would say. "Just live your life for the Lord. That's all I want for you."

Jermaine said those very words to everyone who walked through the doors of God's Hands. And Jack had witnessed a lot of transformations in people. Once their bellies were full and they'd had a good night's sleep, some went right back to the world they'd vowed to leave, but some stayed true to their commitment to God. With the Lord's help, Jack would always be one who stayed true.

"You wanna serve or greet?" asked Jermaine.

Jack didn't have to think about it. He wanted the opportunity to say goodbye to the regulars. "Greet."

Jermaine nodded. "Figured as much." He patted Jack's shoulder. "Don't you head out of here 'til I can say a prayer with you."

"I won't."

While Jermaine headed to the front entrance to welcome the people who came for a warm meal, Jack made his way to the kitchen to give one last hug to the volunteers. After several hugs and handshakes, he spied Stella, Jermaine's wife, scooping servings of pudding into cups. In one swift motion, he dipped his finger into one of the cups, then licked off the chocolate.

Stella gasped, turned and smacked the top of his hand. He laughed, and Stella shook the scoop in front of his face. "Jack Isaacs, what do you think you're doing?"

He sobered. "Come to say goodbye to you before it gets too busy out there."

Tears welled in Stella's eyes, and she shook her head. "I'm glad you're going home to your girls, but I sure will miss you."

Wrapping her in a hug, he said, "I'm gonna miss you, too."

She wiggled away from him, and Jack bit back a grin. Her heart was as big as the state she served, but she didn't like any displays of affection. Scooping up the cup of pudding he'd already sampled, he placed a quick kiss on the top of her head. "We *will* keep in touch."

She swiped her eyes with the back of one hand and shooed him away with the other. "Sure. Sure. Now head on outta here. We got a job to do."

Jack made his way back to the dining area. Several regulars had already filtered into the room. He grinned when he spied Jermaine standing at the front door greeting each homeless person with a kind word and a handshake. He planned to invite people in the same way when he started his position the following week as director of a homeless shelter in Tennessee.

His heartbeat sped up again at the thought of heading back to the Volunteer State. He couldn't wait to see his daughters. So many times over the past two years and ten months he'd longed to hightail it out of Texas, head back to Tennessee and get to know his girls. But he couldn't. He'd had to conquer his addiction, and he'd had to finish school and get a job. Proving to Pamela that he'd changed would be a difficult feat, but he was finally ready to take on the challenge.

In only a few more hours, he'd Skype his younger sister and brother to tell them and his parents goodbye; then he'd hit the road and head toward a life he wished he'd taken advantage of eight years ago. He could never get back those years with Pamela and his girls, but he planned to spend the rest of his life making it up to them.

Chapter 2

Pamela pulled her car behind the long line of vehicles filled with parents waiting to pick up their children after school. She glanced at the clock on the dash. Fifteen minutes until the dismissal bell. She scooped her notebook out of the backpack. Her professor had given a writing assignment she didn't quite understand. While skimming the directions again, she saw a car pull into the side parking lot where the buses lined up.

"He'd better get out of there before Miss Murphy sees him," she mumbled, then grinned at the memory of the elderly guidance counselor pitching a fit to a teenaged girl who'd blocked the buses and caused a fifteen-minute delay.

The man got out of his car and greeted one of the office ladies. The woman motioned toward the parking spaces in front of the building. Pamela furrowed her brows. The guy looked familiar; tall, thin build, red hair. If he'd turn around, maybe she could identify him.

The office lady moved, and the man faced her. Pamela's stomach dropped. It wasn't. It couldn't be. But it was. Plain as day. The husband she hadn't seen in eight years.

Fury swelled inside her as he got back in the small car and drove to the front parking lot. What did he think he was doing here? He had a lot of nerve believing he could come to this school and talk to her children without speaking to her first.

Once he parked, she yanked open the door and raced toward him. She hated the thrill that warred with the fury at seeing him. He looked good. Older. A little more worn for wear but still so handsome he made her heart beat faster.

The smile that brightened his face quickly dropped when she scowled. Crossing her arms in front of her chest, she dug her heels into the ground a few feet away from him. "Just what do you think you're doing here, Jack?"

"Pamela." His voice sounded breathless. The kindness that shone from his eyes made her almost drop her resolve to remain furious. Almost.

"Why are you here?"

"Pamela. You look good." He trailed his fingers through his hair.

A memory of the softness of those curly locks raced through her, and she found herself wanting to touch them once more. It had been so long since she'd seen Jack, and she'd loved him with everything in her all those years ago. How she had wanted him to stop drinking!

Just stop.

She'd given him chance after chance, believing if

she could love him enough he would stop in time. But he hadn't.

Through gritted teeth she spat, "You need to leave. You have no right—"

He lifted his hands in surrender. "I'm not going to say anything to them. I never planned to without your permission." He placed his hands against his chest. "But I want to see them. Just see what they look like. That's all."

"I should call the cops. I could, you know."

"And say what? The father of two students who go to this school wants to see them. I have rights, Pamela."

How dare he? Pamela uncrossed her arms, straightened them to her sides and balled up her fists. He'd left her eight years ago with one baby and pregnant with another and now he wanted to talk about his rights. "I can't believe you just said that."

He furrowed his brows, and Pamela chided herself for longing to touch his cheek and trace her fingers down his jaw. How could she be so angry with him and so drawn to him at the same time?

"I shouldn't have said that." He raked his fingers through his hair again, then balled his fist and tapped it against his forehead. "I wanted the first time I saw you to go differently."

He looked back up at her. Sincerity bore into the depths of her soul through his gaze, and Pamela's knees weakened. Her resolve started to wane. Before she lost it completely, she pointed at him. "Don't say one word to either of them. You and I will have to discuss this later."

Before he could respond, she twirled on her heel and stomped back toward the car. One of the moms waiting in line jumped out of her vehicle and touched Pamela's shoulder. "Everything okay?"

She forced a smile toward Simon's mother. "Just fine. No worries."

"Who is that guy?"

"Just a guy."

Simon's mother twisted the strands of pearls around her neck as she studied Jack. Pamela offered a silent plea to God that the woman would leave her alone. Realizing she was petitioning a being she'd determined to ignore, she grimaced.

"You look upset," said Simon's mother.

Pamela wished she could remember the woman's name. They'd met various times, and she had often talked to Pamela about class activities and field trips, but Pamela wasn't interested in making friends. "Really, I'm fine."

"But—"

Before the woman could continue, the dismissal bell rang. Pamela blew out a sigh of relief when the woman was forced to head back to her car with a quick wave.

She glanced toward Jack. He sat forward in his seat, watching for the girls to make their way from the building. She wished he'd been that eager to see them years ago. Things would have been a lot easier for her if she'd had a husband to lean on.

Emma and Emmy raced toward the car. Emma's tights had a hole at the knee. Emmy, who had started the day with pigtails with bright red bows, now had lopsided ponytails and only one bow in her hair. She also sported a chocolate milk stain on the front of her shirt. *The first time he sees them they look like vagabonds.*

Pamela pushed the concern away. What did she care

what Jack thought? Emma hopped in the backseat and scooted over so Emmy could jump in, as well. They snapped their seat belts, and Pamela asked, "How was school?"

"Good. We made pumpkin puppets," said Emmy.

"And I've got a note about the fall festival," said Emma.

"I got one, too," said Emmy.

"I hope you still have your other red hair bow," said Pamela.

"I do. It's in my bag. Fell out during recess."

Pamela pulled forward in the line. She felt Jack watching them. Pretending she didn't see him, she drove out of the parking lot. "You'll have to show me all your stuff when we get home."

Excitement filled Jack's heart as he drove forty-five minutes back to the homeless shelter where he'd accepted the position as director. The girls looked healthy and happy. And just like their mother—absolutely gorgeous.

Regret weeded through him when he thought of how big they were and how much he had missed. If only he'd gotten sober sooner. He should have given his life to God when he'd had the opportunity as a young person, still in school. Maybe then he wouldn't have gotten messed up with alcohol.

He pushed the "if onlys" away, knowing that harboring them only caused him grief. He couldn't change the past. He had to focus on the present and the future. A future that would include his family.

A smile lifted his lips. It felt good to see them. And Pamela. She'd been so angry when she'd stomped over to the car and when she'd walked away. But there had been moments in their conversation when he'd seen tenderness in her gaze.

And she looked wonderful. He remembered Pamela with long red hair, pulled up with clips on the sides, little to no makeup and a small pooch in her belly for the babe growing inside. Now her hair was cut just past her shoulders with choppy wisps giving it volume. She wore makeup and trendy clothes, looking more mature and beautiful than he remembered.

He pulled into the driveway alongside the aged brick-and-vinyl building. The wooden sign in the front had once read The Refuge. But the elements and no upkeep had washed away the *R* and both *E*s. It would take a lot of elbow grease to get the shelter up to par again, but he didn't mind.

Teresa, a volunteer from the church that had sponsored the reopening of the shelter, met him in the front room. "Hey, Jack, the plumber has already come and gone. The bathroom is good as new."

She motioned for him to follow her to the back. He stepped into the four-stall bathroom and gasped. "Wow! Looks like you've been cleaning, as well."

Teresa blushed. "Well, with the new paint and the new stall doors, it didn't take that much effort to clean it up." She turned on the faucets of both sinks. "And we have running water."

He lifted his hand, and she high-fived it. "That's wonderful. What did he say about the kitchen?"

"He'll be back tomorrow."

"The electrician has completed his work also. Now we just have to get this place cleaned up and pass the city's inspection, and we'll be back in business."

Teresa rubbed her hands together. "And just in time. In October the warmth quickly disappears the further we get into the month."

Jack nodded. "I remember." Sadness tinged his voice.

After walking back into the main room of the building, he rolled up his sleeves, then grabbed a can of paint off the floor. "Anybody else coming to paint today?"

"In an hour or two." She shrugged. "But it's just you and me until then."

Jack bit back his frustration. Teresa was a nice woman, and she'd been instrumental in getting The Refuge back into shape, but she also seemed to have a bit of a crush on him. He couldn't imagine why. She'd been part of the interview process. She knew he had an estranged wife and two children he longed to get to know again. Still, she seemed to like him. Or maybe she was just nice and he didn't know how to handle her kindness. Regardless, being alone with her was the last thing he wanted.

His phone beeped. It was his sister, Kari. He read her text message and grimaced. His mom had been depressed since he'd left, which Kari feared would affect her multiple sclerosis.

Jack sent a quick reply that he would call tonight to talk with Mom. Her sadness at his move made no sense. Since kicking him out for the last time a few years ago, his dad hadn't wanted Jack back in the house. He stayed in touch with the family, but they hadn't seen each other in person in years.

He took the can of paint into the kitchen, popped it open and stirred. After pouring a large amount into a pan, he carried it back into the main room. He dipped the roller into the pan and started painting the wall closest to the door. Maybe if he didn't say anything to Teresa, they could work without any awkward moments.

Several minutes passed and he hadn't heard from Teresa at all. He sneaked a peek out the window. Surely she hadn't left without telling him. Her car was still in the drive, so she was still around somewhere.

As if sensing his thoughts, she walked into the room. "I made some sandwiches for lunch."

Jack started to refuse, but his stomach betrayed him and let out a large growl. He grinned as he placed a hand against his midsection. "Guess I'm ready to take a break."

She smiled back at him and winked. "I'd say so."

He bit the inside of his mouth. "When did you say some of the others were coming?"

She shrugged. "Anytime I guess."

He nodded and lifted his paint-covered hands. "I'll head to the bathroom and wash up."

Lifting a quick prayer to God for the others to hurry up and arrive, he turned on the faucet. His phone rang in the other room. Expecting a call from the inspector, he hollered, "Teresa, that's probably Phil. Will you answer that?"

"Sure."

He hurried through washing his hands, wiped them on a towel and made his way back into the main room. Teresa held out the phone to him, her expression one of stunned confusion. "It's not Phil."

Jack took the phone. "Hello."

"Hi, Jack." Pamela's tone dripped sarcasm. "I wanted to talk with you about today, but if you're busy…"

"Of course I'm not busy, Pamela." He frowned. "How did you get my number?"

"Is it a problem that your wife called you?"

Jack's heart flipped at her mention of the word *wife*. He wanted her to be his wife again, in every way, and the jealousy she felt because another woman had answered the phone warmed him from his head to his toes. "You can call me anytime. I didn't know you had my number."

"It was in the letter."

So she'd written it down. She'd opened the mail, seen the check and letter and written down his number. *Please, God, let her be willing to give me a chance.* "I'm glad you've got it. You can call me anytime you'd like. Day or night. What's up?"

"I wanted to talk about the girls."

"I'd love that. Let me take you to dinner."

"Well, I don't—"

"Please, Pamela."

He heard her sigh over the line. "Fine. I'll meet you at Betty's Diner tomorrow at six."

"Perfect." He gripped the phone tighter, praying Pamela could hear the urgency in his voice. "I can't wait to see you again."

She didn't respond. The phone went dead, but his heart soared with excitement. Tomorrow night had to be perfect.

Chapter 3

The night couldn't have gone any worse. The plumber arrived at The Refuge and found more problems than he'd expected in the kitchen. Jack ended up staying a full hour longer than planned.

The main room was painted and looked nice enough, until he discovered they'd used the bedroom paint, which meant he hadn't had enough for the main room and had to run to the store and purchase another gallon. He didn't feel right about asking the church to pay for his mistake, so it was money from his own account. Money he didn't have.

After racing to his apartment, he jumped in and out of the shower in record time. He opened the dryer door, only to realize he'd forgotten to put the clothes in the washer into the dryer. He growled. The shirt he'd planned to wear to meet Pamela was still wet and he didn't have time to dry it.

He settled on a long-sleeved blue knit shirt and a pair of jeans. Jack rushed through getting dressed and brushing his hair. He looked at the clock on the dash of his car. If he didn't get stopped by lights, he'd make it to the restaurant right on time.

Stopping at the first light, he realized he'd forgotten to put on deodorant. He rolled his eyes and scavenged through the glove compartment. He always kept an extra stick in there. He snapped the glove compartment shut, remembering he'd taken it out to take to the gym.

Trailing his hand through his hair, he blew out a deep breath. *God, calm my nerves. This means so much to me. Don't let me blow it.*

He pulled into the diner's parking lot ten minutes late. With a shrug, he got out of the car. There was nothing he could do about the time. The day had been a mess from the moment he'd hit the alarm clock that morning. He sucked in a deep breath. But it was time for that to change. Maybe his meeting with Pamela would set things right.

He walked into the diner and looked around the room. He didn't see her. Maybe she was running late, as well. A sick feeling swelled in his gut, but he pushed it down. She wouldn't stand him up. It wasn't in Pamela's nature. Since the day he'd met her, she'd attacked things head-on. No playing games. No shying away.

Of course, he hadn't known Pamela for eight years. While he was in the midst of drinking, living with his parents, then with one friend or another, time seemed to go slowly. Like every day was a year. Now that he was sober, he realized just how much he'd missed. Possibly she had changed.

He took a booth near the back of the restaurant, where

he could see the front door. The waitress, a slim blonde girl who couldn't have been more than sixteen, walked up to him. "Ya want something to drink?"

Jack waved his hand. "In a minute. I'm waiting for someone."

The girl nodded. "'Kay. Let me know when you're ready."

Fifteen minutes passed, and Jack pulled out his cell phone and looked at the call from Pamela the day before. If she hadn't blocked her number, he could have called and found out what was going on. But he couldn't. All he could do was wait and pray she'd walk through that door.

The girl returned. "Let me get you something to drink." She pulled a tablet out of the front of her apron and a note fell out. She scooped it off the table and bopped herself on the forehead. "Can't believe I forgot this."

He frowned. "Forgot what?"

She smacked her lips. "And you fit the description the woman gave." She shook her head. "You wouldn't happen to be Jack Isaacs, would ya?"

Jack sat up straight. "Yes."

She exhaled an exaggerated breath. "I'm sorry, mister. I forgot a lady brought this by." She handed him the folded-up note. "I'll get ya whatever ya want. It'll be on the house."

"Anything diet is fine." Jack took the note from her hand. He opened it and immediately recognized Pamela's handwriting.

His heart ached as he read her angry and frustrated words. She had no intention of allowing him to see the girls. None.

He crumpled up the letter in his hand and stared out

the window. Bloom Hollow, Tennessee, was undoubtedly one of the most beautiful places in the world. Orange, salmon, yellow and red leaves covered trees that sat on rolling hills. On this October evening, nature looked especially gorgeous with the setting sun shedding light and warmth on everything in its path.

But the warmth evaded Jack, and darkness threatened to surround him. He craved a drink.

He yanked his wallet from his back pocket and pulled out the small card Jermaine had given him. He'd filled it up with verses of comfort and strength, words to see him through when his alcoholic demons lifted their heads.

He rubbed the card between his thumb and forefinger, then read the words that were already imprinted on his heart. *I will not give in to temptation.* He'd known Pamela might not want anything to do with him at first. He had prepared for that.

Closing his eyes, he lifted a silent prayer to God. How he needed Jermaine's steadiness right now. *God, I know You are with me always. I know that. But I sure would like to have a friend.*

"Well, Jack Isaacs, is that you?"

Jack opened his eyes and spied one of his old drinking buddies, Owen Cundriff. Forcing a smile to his lips, he motioned for him to take a seat across from him. *God, Owen is not who I meant.*

Owen extended his hand across the table, and Jack shook it. "I heard you were back in town. So, how have you been?"

Jack scratched his jaw. "Doing okay. Took a while to get my life straightened out, but I'm sober now."

Owen took his other hand out of his jacket pocket.

In it he held a small, well-worn Bible. Jack looked from the Bible to his friend. Owen smiled. "Guess that makes two of us."

Pamela was the biggest heel on the planet. She shouldn't have chickened out. She should have met Jack at the diner and told him face-to-face that she didn't want him back in her or the girls' lives.

It wasn't that he didn't deserve to be stood up. He deserved plenty worse than that, but she prided herself on being up-front and honest with people, and ditching him was neither.

"Mom! How long are you going to take checking my math paper?" whined Emmy.

Pamela blinked and looked at the assignment she'd been holding in her hand for far too long. "Sorry 'bout that, sweetie."

She focused on the paper and marked the few answers that Emmy had gotten wrong so her younger daughter could redo them. Emmy rolled over on the bed and started fixing the errors. Emma walked into the bedroom, brushing her long, wet hair. "Will you braid it wet so it will be scrunchy in the morning?" she asked.

"Sure." Pamela patted the side of the bed, and Emma plopped down in front of her.

She wondered what the girls would think about their dad. Only on rare occasions had either of them brought him up. She figured it was largely because their grandpa and uncles were such strong male influences in their lives. Still, she wondered if they would want to meet Jack.

"Ow! Mom, you're pulling too tight!" Emma complained.

Pamela loosened her grip. "Sorry."

Emmy shoved the math paper back in her face. "Fixed now?"

Pamela looked cross-eyed, then leaned away from the paper. Spying the two corrections, she nodded her head. "Looks good. Now go get your bath."

"Aw, but I want a snack."

"After your bath. Go."

Emmy pouted, but she didn't complain further as she made her way into the bathroom.

Pamela wrapped a ponytail holder around the bottom of Emma's hair. "Your homework's finished, right?"

"Yep. But I need you to sign the fall festival form."

Emma hopped up and pulled the sheet out of her backpack. Pamela read through the various needs for her class. Someone to work the booth. People to bring snacks and small trinkets. Someone to put together the basket to be raffled. Grabbing the pencil off Emmy's bed, she said, "Guess I'll sign up for cupcakes again."

Emma's shoulders slumped. "I was hoping we could work the booth. I got to help paint it during lunch today."

Pamela looked at the date of the festival again. She didn't have any night classes, so she should be able to make it. She grinned and pulled Emma into a hug. "Okay. We'll do the booth." She pointed to Emmy's backpack. "Get her bag, too. I'm sure I need to sign up for something for her."

After signing Emmy's paper and brushing through her hair once she'd gotten out of the shower, Pamela took the girls to the kitchen for a snack. Bedtime took over an hour every night, and she was always exhausted by the time the girls were nestled into their beds.

Tonight, she still had a couple loads of laundry, which was a challenge because she had to lug the clothes to the B and B since she didn't have a washer and dryer in the cabin. Sure, it was only twenty or so yards to the main house, but it was still a pain. Plus, she had her own homework to do.

Jack drifted through her mind. If he had never left, she'd have someone to lean on, to help her with all the daily chores that went with having children. Now he pleaded to be allowed back into her life, into the lives of her children. She couldn't deny the check he'd tried to give her would help out in many ways.

But she couldn't do it. Money usually came with strings attached, and she didn't trust him. What if she let him back in their lives and then he started drinking again? What would that do to the girls? She shook her head. No. She couldn't risk it.

Once the girls finished their snack, she guided them to their bedroom and listened while they said their prayers. Their innocent faith was sweet, and she wished she could protect them from the cruelty they would one day encounter in the world. Part of her wished she could go back to a time of such childlike innocence. But adult life wasn't like that. Responsibilities weighed far heavier, and God had failed her more times than she'd have ever imagined He would.

With the girls tucked in, Pamela made the short trek to the main house. She threw a load of clothes in the washing machine and started it. She opened the door to head back to the cabin.

"Pamela, will you come here a minute?" her mom called from the living area. Pamela walked in there to find her mom and dad sitting on the couch. Dread filled her when she noticed they held hands. She braced herself for bad news. "What is it?"

"We got a phone call today." Her mom placed her hand against her chest. "I can't even begin to tell you how surprised we were. It was so unexpected." Mom gazed at Dad, who nodded in agreement.

Fury washed over her. She knew who had called them. Swallowing back her emotions, she nodded. "Okay."

"It was Jack."

She bit the inside of her mouth, willing herself not to throw a fit right in front of her parents.

"You don't seem surprised," said her dad.

She lifted her chin. "I'm not."

"He wants to meet with us." Tammie's voice was a little above a whisper, and Pamela couldn't decipher the expression on her face.

"We told him he could come here for lunch tomorrow," Mike said.

Pamela blinked several times as she peered at her parents. "Why would you tell him that?"

Her dad stood and walked toward her. He placed his hand on Pamela's shoulder, but she pulled away. "He says he's clean. Finished his degree. Even has a good job. I called around after we got off the phone with him. He seems to be telling the truth."

Pamela looked away from her parents. She couldn't believe they would betray her this way. "Doesn't mean he won't go back."

"We want to talk with him. It's the right thing to do. It's what God would—"

"Don't talk to me about God!" Pamela marched out of the house. She didn't care that she sounded like a spoiled teenager as she slammed the sturdy door shut. She hated the bitterness she felt, the deep-to-her-core fear that Jack would walk back into her life and trample her heart all over again. It was not her parents' place to meet with Jack. He was her husband, and the girls were hers. Not theirs. Just one more reason she could not wait to be on her own completely.

Chapter 4

Jack stepped out of the car, then tucked the bottom of his flannel shirt into his good pair of jeans. He'd forgotten about the splattering of paint on the bottom of the shirt. He should have remembered! He needed to make a good impression on Mike and Tammie. They were giving him a chance, and he had to make the most of it. Sucking in a deep breath, he remembered his and Owen's prayer for God's blessing on this visit. He had to trust in God's grace and not worry about flannel shirts and paint.

Raking his fingers through his hair, he allowed his gaze to take in Jacobs Family Farm. It was just as it had always been. The white bed-and-breakfast looked inviting with the yellow-and-orange mums, pumpkins of various sizes and happy scarecrows surrounding the wooden sign that welcomed guests. He could see the edge of the small cabin behind the B and B, the white farmhouse to the right, along with the gift shop and café, the activity center and petting zoo. The apple and peach trees to the left seemed to go on forever, and his mouth watered at a sudden memory of Pamela's homemade apple crisps. The family had always raved over her strawberry pies, and they were amazingly delicious, to be sure, but her apple crisps...

Jack licked his lips. He could almost feel the warmth of the apple, the crunch of the granola. Could almost taste the perfect mixture of sugar and cinnamon, the apples, tart and yet sweet. He cupped his hand over his mouth, then ran his fingers from his cheeks to his jaw.

He drank in the rolling mountains behind the property, adorned in yellows, oranges, reds and greens. Blowing out a breath, he willed his pounding heart to slow down. It was like God had picked up paint and brush and created a masterpiece of warmth and comfort in those Tennessee mountains. His mind replayed walks with Pamela through that land. Times he'd held her hand, kissed her lips, her neck...

He shuddered. He hadn't anticipated such a strong reaction to the place. His throat felt dry and coarse. He needed a drink. Water.

As he curled his fingers tighter around the keys, unworthiness washed over him. He didn't deserve to try to have this again. This life. This family. Pamela and his girls. He'd thrown it away. Worse than that—he'd ignored and trampled the gift God had given him.

I can't do this, God.

He grabbed the car door handle.

"Jack, is that you?"

He looked to the house and spied Tammie standing on the porch. Eight years could have been eight days. She hadn't changed a bit. Dark hair rested on her shoulders. She wore a green sweatshirt and jeans. Her expression was kind and caring as ever. Mike stepped out of the house. He had more salt in his salt-and-pepper hair, but other than that, he'd changed as little as Tammie.

Mike waved for him to join them. "Well, come on up here, son. Let's have a look at you."

Son? How could Mike say that? Jack had left their daughter and two grandbabies.

The Spirit nudged him to just trust Him, and Jack put one foot in front of the other. Somehow he made it to the porch. He took Mike's extended hand in his. Before words could leave his mouth, Tammie had enveloped him in a hug.

"It's good to see you again."

Jack swallowed back the tears threatening to spill down his cheeks. Why would they be nice to him? How could she so willingly embrace him? "You have no idea how good it is to see you two, as well."

She released him, and Mike patted his shoulder. "Let's go inside and talk."

Jack nodded as he followed them inside. The living room looked just as he remembered. Old-fashioned, homey furnishings, the smell of cinnamon. The land, the house, his in-laws…only days could have passed rather than years.

Until he scanned the walls and tables covered with pictures of his daughters at various ages. Proof that more than a day or two had slipped out of his grasp.

"Why don't you look at the pictures while Mike and I get the sandwiches and chips?"

Jack moved toward the fireplace. He bit his bottom lip at the photo of the girls smiling cheesy grins, probably three and four, sitting at a small table. The next photo was of them and Pamela sitting in front of the Christmas tree. Emmy was just a baby. Emma not much bigger. Pamela was smiling, but she seemed tired. Alone.

He looked away and spied pictures of the girls with Pamela's brothers, Kirk and Ben. Emma sat on Kirk's shoulders. Emmy on Ben's. They were dressed in red-and-white outfits and had probably been heading to Bloom Hollow's annual Fourth of July celebration.

"They're beautiful girls."

Jack started at Tammie's words. He turned toward her and Mike as they set a tray of food on the coffee table. "They look like their mother."

"They do," said Mike. He motioned toward the food. "Go ahead and get yourself a plate."

Jack placed a ham-and-cheese sandwich, chips and a pickle on his plate and sat in the wingback chair. He lifted the sandwich to his mouth, then placed it back on the plate. "I need to talk first."

"Okay," said Tammie. Her gaze was kind, open to whatever he had to share.

"What do you need to tell us?" said Mike.

"Everything."

With the one word came a waterfall of confessions. He shared about his battle with alcoholism, of bouncing from his parents' home to friends' homes until he finally ended up in a homeless shelter in Texas.

"It was the night the woman showed up there with her two daughters. The woman's eyes were blackened. The girls were cold and terrified."

Jack swallowed, trying to shake away the vision that still plagued him at times. He thought of the night Pamela told him to leave the house. He was drunk, yelling at her, and he'd come close. So close to… He couldn't even think the words. Wouldn't allow them to form in his mind.

"When I saw that woman and those girls, I became physically ill, knowing they could have been my girls. I cried out to God. Jermaine was there. He prayed with me. Became my mentor. He's the one who helped me get back in school. Gave me the job at the shelter. Accepted me as a friend."

Tammie swiped a tear from her cheek. She and Mike held hands and leaned toward each other.

Jack went on, sharing about the past three years, the changes he'd made in his life, going back to school, living and working at the shelter, even calling Pamela and hanging up.

Glancing at the clock, he realized two hours had passed. He had to get back to the shelter for a meeting with the pastor of the sponsoring church. He handed them the check Pamela had sent back to him.

Mike took it, then grabbed Jack in a hug. "We never stopped praying for you."

Tammie wrapped her arms around both of them. "And we won't now. We'll be praying for you and Pamela."

"Thank you." Remembering Pamela's anger at seeing him at the school, he knew only God could help Pamela forgive him.

Pamela's leg wouldn't stop shaking. She doodled another star on the edge of the notepad, then crossed her left leg over her right. *Concentrate. You need to know this stuff.*

She straightened her back and lifted her chin, determined to hear the words droning from the professor's mouth. Why did financial management have to be so boring? Glancing at her cell phone, she wondered if Jack was still at the house. She bit back a growl of frustration that her parents would consider speaking with him.

After uncrossing her legs, she curled her right foot around the left, then tucked them both under the chair. She simply could not sit still. Noting the glare from the dark-haired guy to her left, Pamela offered a faint smile, then grabbed her purse and walked out of the room.

She released the growl once the door shut behind her. Lifting the purse strap onto her shoulder, she stalked to the ladies' restroom. Jack infuriated her. Her parents infuriated her. What were they thinking meeting with him after all this time? They, of all people, knew what she'd gone through when he left. The exhaustion. The tears. The loneliness.

She wet a paper towel with cold water, then dabbed her cheeks and forehead. She had to get a handle on her emotions. After throwing away the towel, she scavenged through her purse for change. Maybe if she bought a pack of gum from the lounge, she could keep her jitters at bay by chewing a piece, or the whole pack. Whatever it took.

With change in hand, she spied the vending machine and selected a flavor. After popping a piece in her mouth, she swallowed a quick drink from the water fountain to cool the fiery cinnamon taste. She stood to her full height. *Pamela Isaacs, you can do this. March right back in that room. Take notes, and stop thinking about Jack.*

"Pamela, how are you?"

She turned at the deep voice of one of her professors from two semesters ago. If ever there was a man who could tempt her to consider falling in love again, Dr. Peter Dane was the guy. Dark hair fell in one perfect wave to the left on his forehead. Brilliant blue eyes glistened above a five-o'clock shadow that covered a strong jawline. Though a bit on the short side, broad shoulders and a muscular frame made up for any concerns about his height.

"Dr. Dane, you remembered my name." Her cheeks warmed. Her tongue had gotten tangled up with the gum and she'd spit out the words. Literally.

"You're a poet and didn't know it." He laughed. "Of course I'd remember you."

Warmth raced from her cheeks down her neck at the sudden intensity of his expression. "I'm actually in class right now." She pointed to her mouth. "Just needed a little help to stay focused."

"What class are you taking?"

"Financial Management."

He cringed. "Dr. Mays?"

She nodded.

"Yep. A challenge to stay awake, let alone concentrate."

She nodded again. He didn't say anything else, and Pamela couldn't think or move. She focused on the slight dark curl at the base of his neck.

"Well, maybe we could meet after your class. Get a late lunch."

Pamela gripped the purse strap. He couldn't be asking her on a date. "I have to pick up my girls from school."

He snapped his fingers. "I remember. Emma and Emmy, right?"

She nodded once more. He remembered her girls' names? She hadn't seen Dr. Dane in months and couldn't recall that she'd made more than a handful of comments in his class. Sure, all the students filled out an information form at the beginning of the semester, but for him to remember her daughters…

Pamela didn't know how to respond.

He grinned and leaned closer. "Maybe another time." Her heart stopped beating when he whispered, "At least now I know where to find you. Dr. Mays's financial management class."

He turned and walked away. Dumbstruck, Pamela blinked and watched him go. What had just happened? Surely, her ultracute professor wasn't interested in her. But what if he was?

She and Jack had never divorced. She'd never sought him out for one. For years, part of her had hoped one day he would clean up his act and come back to her. Those hopes had died away soon enough. Returning to college had given her an independence she hadn't realized she'd missed so desperately.

She wasn't quite nineteen when Emma was born, and Emmy joined them just one year and a day later. Pamela hadn't known independence at all until she'd gone back to school. Now she relished it. Soon she wouldn't need her parents' help. She most assuredly didn't need to pine after Jack. And Dr. Peter Dane was gorgeous with a capital *G*.

Now that she knew where Jack was, maybe the time had come to ask for a divorce. It wasn't as if they'd had any semblance of a marriage the past eight years. And abandonment was biblical grounds, wasn't it? Not that she cared what God thought. At least, she didn't want to care. She headed back toward the classroom. It was something to think about.

Chapter 5

"So, what did you think of the service?"

Jack sat in the chair across from Owen and his wife, Karen. "The sermon was terrific. The pastor spoke the truth. No mincing of words. I like that."

Owen picked up the menu. "Yeah, and I can relate to the apostle Paul and the whole trying not to do what I want to do."

Jack took a drink of water. "Fighting our natural desires is not an easy thing."

"Yeah, like the temptation to order one of the diner's famous cheeseburgers and fries instead of the chicken salad and diet soft drink," Karen said as she placed her and Owen's young son in the high chair.

Owen chuckled. "I don't know if I'd put the temptation of food in the same category as alcohol."

"Why not?" Karen lifted a cracker out of the diaper bag and handed it to Wyatt. The toddler cackled and clapped his hands before taking the treat. "We all have battles, and mine plagues me, as well."

"True," said Jack. "But overeating won't land you in a homeless shelter."

"But it can land you in the hospital." Karen pulled out her wallet and handed Jack a photo. "That was me in high school."

Jack raised his eyebrows at the picture of a teenager double Karen's size.

"I was fifteen years old and a borderline diabetic."

Jack handed the picture back to her. "What did you do?"

She pointed to both of them. "Just like you two, I surrendered to the Lord. Then I got some help from a dietician, joined a gym with an accountability partner and worked with a vengeance to get healthy."

A woman with long brown hair pulled back in a braid walked up to the table to take their orders. Jack had planned to get the cheeseburger and fries, then thought of the apostle Paul's admonition to never be a stumbling block to a brother or sister. He handed the menu to the waitress. "I'll take the chicken salad and a regular soft drink."

When the woman walked away, Karen shook her head. "Jack, you could have ordered the burger you said you wanted when we pulled up."

"Would you have ordered a beer in front of Owen and me?"

Owen chortled and pointed to his wife. "She's never even touched the stuff."

She looked from Owen back to Jack. "No. I wouldn't."

"Which is why I didn't get the cheeseburger."

Owen draped his arm over Karen's shoulder. "And

why I don't get the cheeseburger—" he pointed toward Jack "—unless I'm with someone like this guy."

Karen wrinkled her nose. "Encouragement feels good." Wyatt squalled, and she handed him another cracker. "I'm glad you've moved back here, Jack. You and Owen will be good for each other."

The front door of the restaurant opened, and Pamela and their daughters walked in, followed by Mike, Tammie, Kirk and Callie. Jack's heart raced at the sight of his girls. Emma was so tall, and he could see Emmy's dimples from across the room as she laughed at something Kirk said.

They didn't see him, and Jack contemplated whether he should wave or simply watch. When the hostess seated them on the other side of the diner, he decided to watch. Emmy sat with her back to him, but Emma sat beside her mother, facing him. He couldn't believe how much alike they looked. It was like seeing Pamela in elementary school all over again.

Someone said something, and they all laughed. Jack bit his lip, wishing he could go over there. Maybe he should. It wouldn't be so bad. He had the right to see his daughters.

"Don't do it, man."

Jack blinked, his thoughts focusing again on the people in front of him. He looked at Owen and furrowed his brows. "What?"

Owen glanced over his shoulder. "Not yet. You gotta talk with Pamela first."

"The girls might not even know you're in Tennessee," added Karen.

Pamela looked his way. Their gazes locked. At first her expression lifted, and he thought she might smile.

Then she squinted and a scowl marked her face. She stood and walked toward the restrooms. Jack stood, as well.

"Man, don't."

Jack glanced down at Owen. "I think she wants me to follow her."

"I'm not so sure that's—"

Jack didn't wait for Karen to finish her sentence. He walked to the back of the diner and waited outside the ladies' restroom. Pamela opened the door. Anger and bitterness filled her face in a way he'd never seen. She spat through gritted teeth, "If we'd known you were here, we wouldn't have come."

Somehow he had to make her see he was a different man. That he'd never again hurt her or the girls. That God controlled his life, not the bottle.

He thought of the conversation with Owen and Karen from only moments ago. For the rest of his life, he'd battle the bottle, but each day he stayed surrendered to God the temptation weakened. And Pamela and the girls could be additional encouragement. "Pamela, I—"

"Jack, you're not listening." She pointed to her ear. "I don't care what you have to say. My own parents want me to talk to you, but I don't care."

His heart skipped when he heard Mike and Tammie had been talking to her, that they wanted to give him a second chance.

"I'm different. I want you. I want—"

She lifted her hand. "You have no right to want me." She crossed her hands in front of her chest, then swiped them to each side. "None."

Bitter contempt radiated from her with such certainty, he took a step back. He loved Pamela. He wanted her as his wife again, but he'd have to start with the girls. She had to listen to him at least on that account. Any judge would side with him if he paid child support and stayed sober, and he had every intention of doing both. "The girls. I have the right to see them."

"You have no right. And if you step one foot toward our table, I will scoop up *my* children and walk out of this restaurant."

He felt as if he'd been punched in the gut as she stomped back toward the table. He heard Emmy ask her what was wrong. Pamela plastered a smile on her face. Sadness swallowed him as he shoved both fists in his jeans pockets. He could follow her, introduce himself to his daughters and demand the right to spend time with them, but that would put a rip between Pamela and him that might never be mended. *God, what do I do?*

Pamela balled her fists and pressed her knuckles against the kitchen counter. She'd spent the past half hour arguing with her parents about Jack. He was the alcoholic who'd left her alone with two daughters, so why was she the bad guy?

The memory of that night eight years ago swept over her. Jack's eyes, bloodshot and glassy, peered at her with malice that sent tremors of fear down her spine.

Emma had been sick, throwing up all over the place, and Pamela was only a few months pregnant with Emmy. The smell and sight of Emma's vomit sent Pamela to the bathroom. Jack was left to clean up after their daughter. Disoriented, he slipped and fell in the mess. He'd been angry. Cursed. Jumped up. Pulled back his hand at the toddler. Pamela screamed before he could act, and his fury focused on her.

For a long moment, time stood still. He wanted to hit her. The desire was etched in every muscle in his face. Somehow she mustered the courage to tell him to leave the house. He'd grabbed a few things, and that was it. He was gone. And he didn't even try to come back.

Pamela sucked in a deep breath, lifted her chin and peered up at the ceiling. *But I'm the bad guy because I don't want to give him a second chance.* Her parents hadn't been there that night. They hadn't seen the look in his eyes.

It was true he'd never hit her or Emma, and deep in Pamela's gut, she knew her parents would never consider taking a chance if he'd abused them. She remembered the night when Emmy was a newborn and Emma wouldn't sleep. Pamela had been so tired and sore that she'd come close to lashing out at Emma, but she hadn't. She'd stopped herself, just as Jack had stopped.

I've changed. His words echoed through her mind. She'd loved him with every ounce of her being. When he wasn't drinking, he'd been all she'd dreamed. They'd prayed together, studied God's word together, vowed to live their lives for Him. *A lot of good that did.*

She pushed away from the counter and raked her fingers through her hair. She needed a trim. After talking with the girls about their dad, she'd need some pampering time.

He has the legal right to see his children. Her father's words pricked her mind. *And a judge won't turn him down if he's sending money, as well.* Her mom had piped in.

Ugh. How it infuriated her that she had to have this conversation with her girls. He'd walked out of their lives, and she and the girls had done well, were doing well, and then he up and decided to traipse back to Bloom Hollow, sober and ready to reconcile. It wasn't fair. He shouldn't be able to flip their lives upside down whenever he saw fit.

Quit stalling. Just get it over with.

She walked into the living room. Emmy sat on the floor with her favorite panda bear propped against the couch. She'd folded several papers in half and was illustrating a book she'd written. Emma was sprawled on the couch playing a game on the iPad. Pamela settled into her favorite leather recliner. "Girls, I need to talk with you."

"Give me a sec," said Emma.

Pamela didn't mind. She'd give them as long as they wanted. Emma feverishly pressed the tablet's screen. Emmy put the finishing touch on a purple-and-green critter she'd created.

Emmy lifted the paper. "This is my *main* character, Albie. Do you like him?"

Pamela grinned and nodded at her younger daughter. The child loved learning about writing, something Pamela never understood. Numbers made sense. They formed patterns. They were definite. Writing, not so much.

"'Kay. I'm done." Emma set the tablet in her lap and sat up straighter on the couch.

Pamela clasped her hands together. "Well, I need to talk to you both."

Emma clicked her tongue. "You already said that."

Pamela peered at her older child. Only nine and already Emma tried to retort with smart-aleck comments. To Emma's credit, she ducked her chin and appeared repentant under Pamela's glare. "It's about your dad."

"Our dad?" Emmy furrowed her brows.

"You never talk about our dad," said Emma.

"I saw a picture of him once." Emmy sat up straighter. "In one of Grandma's photo albums. He was holding Emma and looking at her with goofy eyes." Her face fell. "But I didn't see one with me."

"That's 'cause he left before you were born," Emma snapped.

"I know," Emmy retorted. "Grandma told me, and—"

Pamela lifted her hand. "Enough. He lives in Tennessee again and wants to meet you."

Emmy's eyes lit up. "Really?"

"Do we have to?" Emma pursed her lips together and frowned.

Pamela studied her older daughter. She looked angrier than Pamela had expected. "I'm not sure, and I don't know how I feel about it, and—"

"I want to meet him, Mom." Emmy stood up, then hopped into Pamela's lap. "I always wanted a mom and dad just like my friends. I mean, Sarah only has a mom like me, but..."

Without a word, Emma wiped a single tear from her cheek, stood and walked to her room. Her child's bitterness cut like a dagger through Pamela's heart. She traced her fingers through Emmy's hair as the girl continued to prattle on about the various students in her class. But worry niggled at Pamela's heart for Emma. How long had her girl been in such pain, and why hadn't she noticed?

Chapter 6

Jack waited in the small office space at The Refuge while the health inspector checked the kitchen. If the shelter passed, they could open the doors the following week. He thumbed through the list of people from Faith Church who had signed up as volunteers, hoping to call them in the next few days to set up schedules.

The front door opened, and Teresa walked in. Jack worried the inside of his mouth. She was a pretty woman, dark hair, dark eyes, had a nice personality. But he didn't feel comfortable when she showed up at the center and he was alone. He didn't want people to get the wrong impression. He didn't want *her* to get the wrong impression. This time the health inspector was there, but he would be leaving.

Jack forced a smile to his lips. "Good afternoon, Teresa."

A blush spread across her cheeks, and Jack wished

he knew how to make her understand his interest rested in his wife and daughters. *Even if Pamela looks ready to wring my neck each time she sees me.*

She twisted the gold stud earring in her earlobe. "I just stopped by on my lunch break to see what the health inspector said."

Jack held back a sigh of relief. If she was on a break, she wouldn't be able to stay long. He pointed toward the kitchen area. "He's still here. Been here awhile, so I assume we'll know soon."

"Oh." She clasped her hands. "I figured he'd be gone. I mean, I'd planned to see if you wanted to grab some lunch, but I don't have a lot of time, and—"

He shook his head. "I don't think that would be a good idea." He lifted his left hand and pointed to his wedding band. "I'm married, and I wouldn't want—"

"I know, but…" She shifted her weight from one foot to the other.

"I love my wife, and I won't do anything to make her think otherwise."

Teresa started to say something, then clamped her lips shut. In one swift movement, she turned on her heels and walked out the door. Jack grinned. He did love his wife, and he was committed to winning her back.

The inspector walked out of the kitchen. "Everything looks great. You and the church have done a good job getting this old place back in working order. I'll email the papers to you, and you can open for business whenever you're ready."

Jack gripped the burly man's hand. "That's terrific. Thanks for your help."

After guiding the inspector out of the shelter, Jack pulled his cell phone out of his pocket and called Jermaine. A deep "hello" boomed over the line, and Jack was surprised at how much he missed his longtime mentor and friend. "It's Jack."

"Jack!" Jermaine's laugh vibrated. "It's good to hear from you, son. How are things?"

"The Refuge just passed its last inspection. I can open for business next week."

"Praise the Lord. What a blessing!"

Jack heard Stella's "hallelujah" in the background, and he knew she was listening to their conversation. He missed getting his hand slapped for sampling one of her dishes before they were ready to serve to their homeless guests.

"How are things with Pamela and the girls?"

Jack frowned. "Not good. She hasn't let me meet them yet, and she won't talk to me."

Jermaine's voice deepened. "Give her some time."

"I'm trying, but I want to see my girls. I want to talk to them. They're my children, too."

"If you go at your wife saying those words, you'll never get her back. Gotta let God do His work."

Jack let out a slow breath. He could recall the number of times Jermaine had said that. When the shelter ran out of food with over a week before funds became available again. When one of the ovens busted, and the shelter had no money to fix it. *Gotta let God do His work* always slipped from Jermaine's lips. And every time, God took care of them.

"You're right. Just keep praying for us."

"Every day," said Jermaine.

"Every day," echoed Stella.

Jack grinned. "And give Stella a kiss for me. Tell her I miss her."

He heard the huff and knew Stella had swatted the air and walked out of the room. Jack chuckled. "I appreciate you, Jermaine."

"I know you do. Hang in there."

"I will."

After saying goodbye, Jack shoved his phone back in his jeans pocket. He grabbed the car keys off the desk. He couldn't wait to tell Pastor Mark they could open the doors on Monday.

Pamela shoved the graded test into the folder. She'd studied for hours for that exam and still failed. She wasn't surprised by the results. The test had been ridiculous. It didn't show whether she understood the material in the book. Instead, Dr. Mays seemed to take whatever section suited his fancy and wanted the students to spit back exact phrases from the text. How did that prove she'd learned anything? It only showed she could memorize. Which obviously she was not able to do, considering she'd gotten a big fat F on the test.

Dr. Mays hadn't even stayed around after class long enough to allow her to talk with him about her grade. She wasn't the only one struggling, and she assumed he simply wanted to get away from the mass of questions. Yanking her calculator out of the bag, she crunched numbers for upcoming assignments. The best she could get in the class now was a B, and that was highly unlikely given her track record of grades on his assignments. *God, what am I gonna do?*

The thought slipped from her mind, and she shook her head. No sense petitioning Him. God had proven time and again that she was living life on her own. He'd even upped the drama by sticking Jack back in her world.

I gotta get a B, or I'll lose my scholarship. She'd worked hard the first year of college to earn the academic scholarship, but her grades had to stay at a certain grade point average in order to keep it.

After shoving the calculator, book and folder in her bag, she got up from the desk. She'd have to email the professor later, ask what she could do to help her grade. Taking a deep breath, she raked her hand through her hair. *I've got a more pressing situation to deal with first.*

She hefted the bag and her purse onto her shoulder. Her gut twisted with humiliation. She'd had to cash Jack's check. Her car had been on its last leg for a year, and a few days ago the transmission had finally croaked. Before class started she'd secured a ride to go pick it up. A ride from Dr. Peter Dane.

Her heartbeat kicked up a notch as she walked out the classroom door and spied her former professor leaning against the doorjamb of his classroom, his gaze trained on the paper in his hand. The guy was simply too cute. And she'd practically jumped out of her skin when he'd offered to drop her off at the mechanic's shop after overhearing her tell her mom on the phone that she needed a ride.

"Hi." The single word slipped through her lips, sounding more breathless than she'd intended. Her heart flipped when he looked up at her and smiled.

"Hey. You ready to go?"

He jangled the keys in his hands, and Pamela nodded. For the briefest of moments she felt wrong, like she was cheating on Jack. She blew out a breath as she followed Peter to his car. *A girl can't cheat on a guy who left her pregnant and penniless years ago.*

Her purse seemed heavier when she thought of the

large sum of money she'd put in the bank that morning. Her parents' insistence that she give Jack a chance hammered at her mind. He didn't deserve a chance.

Peter opened the car door for her, and she slipped inside. Her hands felt clammy as she realized she hadn't been in the car with a man who wasn't her dad, brother or husband in over a decade.

"Where we going?" Peter's voice was smooth, soft, and Pamela willed herself to settle down.

"A & J's."

"On Court Street?"

"Yes."

Pamela buckled her seat belt, then gripped the straps of her bag and purse as Peter pulled out of the parking lot and onto the main road. She cleared her throat. "Thanks so much for giving me a ride."

"My pleasure. I'm glad to see you outside of the college. Wouldn't mind to do it again under different circumstances."

Pamela smiled, but words didn't form on her lips. Part of her wouldn't mind getting to know the professor better. But what would the girls think? Her family? Jack? She blinked. It didn't matter what Jack thought.

Peter pulled into A & J's parking lot and turned off the car. Shifting toward her, he placed his hand on top of hers. Pamela didn't feel the electricity she remembered with Jack; instead dread and guilt washed over her. "I'd really like to take you to dinner sometime, Pamela."

Pamela opened her mouth to respond. She wanted to say yes. Of course. But the words didn't form. The sounds of bells filled the car, and Pamela grabbed her phone from her purse. The school's number showed up on the screen, and she lifted her pointer finger to Peter as she answered the call.

"Hi. Is this Mrs. Isaacs?"

Though Pamela had never changed her married name, renewed guilt washed over her hearing the woman call her missus while she sat in the car with another man who'd just asked her on a date. "Yes. This is she."

"I'm sorry to have to call you, Mrs. Isaacs. This is Karen Williams, the school nurse. I'm afraid Emmy has lice, and we'll need you to come pick her up if at all possible."

Pamela's mouth dropped at the woman's words. She'd never dealt with lice, but she knew a whole lot of cleaning lay ahead of her. Closing her eyes, she sighed when she thought of all the homework she had due the next day. "Okay. I'll be right over."

She pushed End on the phone and turned toward Peter. "Thank you for the ride, and I really appreciate the offer. We'll have to talk about it later, though. I have to pick up my daughter from school."

Concern lifted his brows. "Is everything all right? Do you need my help?"

Pamela wrinkled her nose as she imagined his reaction if she asked him to help her delouse her home. Shaking her head, she said, "No, but thanks anyway."

She got out of the car and walked into the shop. By the time she'd paid for the repairs and walked back outside, Peter had gone. Weariness and frustration welled inside her. She didn't have the energy for lice, and she most certainly didn't have time for it.

Aggravated, she yanked her phone out of her bag. *Jack Isaacs wants to meet his girls. He wants to be back in their lives. Play husband and daddy. Well, now sounds like as good a time as any.* She called his number. Her heart skipped a beat when she heard his greeting.

"Hello?" he said the word again.

"Jack, it's Pamela."

"Pamela."

The way he said her name, like a kiss pressed against her lips, sent shivers down her spine. Lifting her chin, she forced herself to remember the purpose of the call. "You want to see your girls?"

"Yes."

"Then come on over in an hour. You can help me out tonight."

"Really?"

He sounded excited, and Pamela knew her lips were curled into a Cheshire cat grin. "Just don't wear anything nice."

Chapter 7

Jack had just gotten off the phone with his mother when Pamela called. His mom hadn't felt well for quite some time, and he worried about her. Especially when her multiple sclerosis flared up, which it had. His fourteen-year-old sister, Kari, took care of their mom most of the time, while his younger brother, Todd, threw all his concern and energy into his running. Jack's dad still barely talked to him, and Jack prayed their relationship would one day be mended.

He rubbed his hands together as he stepped onto the cabin's porch. The cabin had been a bit of an eyesore when he and Pamela had first married. Now it was fixed up with a swing on the front porch and red curtains in the windows. *God, give me the words to say.*

Conjuring every ounce of courage he could muster, he knocked. He spied Emma peeking through the window on his left. When she saw him, she dropped the curtain, and he heard her run away from the door.

Several minutes passed, and Jack found himself thankful for the warm temperature. He couldn't blame Emma for running away. In her eyes, he was a complete stranger. Guilt gnawed at him, threatened to fill him with self-contempt. *God, help me not to start beating myself up. I can't take back the past. I have only the present and future.*

The door opened, and Jack looked down at his younger daughter. She was beautiful. Long red hair pulled up in a ponytail. Freckles splattering her nose and cheeks. Sparkling blue eyes. Dimples in her cheeks. Jack bit back the urge to scoop her up in his arms and squeeze her until he'd gotten his fill. Instead, he nodded hesitantly. "Hi, Emmy."

She cocked her head and squinted at him. "Are you my dad?"

"I am."

She motioned for him to come inside. "Then come on. Mom's got a bunch of stuff for you to do."

Jack bit back a chuckle as he followed her inside. Pamela walked around the corner, pushing the vacuum with one hand and holding rags and liquid cleaner in the other. Her hair was pulled back with a bandanna, and she wore an old pair of overalls that he remembered from when they dated. She was breathtaking.

A flicker of relief shone through her gaze, but it was soon covered with disdain. Why had she called him if she didn't want him here? To clean obviously, but the place looked well kept already.

She looked from Emma to Emmy. "Girls, this is Jack Isaacs. He's your father."

Emma peeked around the corner, then shuffled toward her mother. Emmy walked up to him and shook his hand. "I'm really glad to meet you. I've wanted a dad for a long time."

Jack swallowed the knot in his throat. "And I've wanted to be your dad a long time, too."

Pamela cleared her throat. "Emma, shake your dad's hand."

Emma's eyes widened, and she gripped the vacuum cleaner's handle. Jack lifted his hands. "It's okay. You can wait until you feel comfortable."

Pamela placed the cleaner and the rags on the couch, then rubbed her hands together. "Well, Jack, you wanted back in our lives. Today seems the perfect day."

He bit his bottom lip, feeling nervous and excited. "What's up?"

She pointed to their younger daughter. "Emmy has lice. I have some lice shampoo in the bathroom, and you get to help me make sure everything is bug-free."

"Actually, mayonnaise is better."

Pamela scowled. "What?"

"Mayonnaise suffocates the lice and nits, and it's much better for her hair."

Pamela squinted. "How would you know that?"

Jack recalled the many times he'd treated his hair at the shelter. One day he would share all that with Pamela, but for now they needed to get started. He pointed to the kitchen. "Do you have mayonnaise?"

"Yes."

"Why don't you put some in both the girls' hair, and I'll strip the beds and—"

"I want you to do my hair." Emmy grabbed his hand in hers and swung it back and forth.

Jack's heart flipped with excitement.

Pamela pointed to Emma. "We'll take care of the beds." She looked at Emmy. "Take him into the kitchen and show him the mayonnaise."

While he rubbed mayonnaise into her hair, Emmy talked to him about homework, her friends, her favorite toys, even the stray dog that roamed around the school at times. He drank in each word, cherished each story.

Every few minutes, he spied Emma and Pamela taking sheets and clothes to the main house. He caught Emma watching him at one point while she stuffed animals into garbage bags. She quickly looked away, and he wished his older daughter would talk with him. But he'd have to give her time.

"Our school's fall festival is on Friday. You wanna come?" asked Emmy.

Before Jack could respond, Emma raced into the room and yelled, "He can't come!"

"Why not?" whined Emmy.

Emma balled her fists. Pamela walked out of a bedroom. "What's wrong?" She put her hand on Emma's shoulder. "Why are you upset?"

Emmy pointed to her own chest. "I want Dad to go to the fall festival."

"No." The word slipped through Emma's gritted teeth.

Pamela glanced at him, her eyebrows raised.

God, what do I say? Of course I'll go to the festival. But Emma?

Pamela knelt down in front of Emma. "If Emmy would like your dad to go to the festival, it will be okay. He can take her to the different activities while you and I work the game for your class."

Emma didn't look at him, and her jaw set in a firm line as she said, "Grandma can take Emmy."

Jack's heart broke. Maybe he should just walk out. In all the scenarios he had dreamed up when he met the girls, he hadn't considered one of them embracing him with open arms and the other loathing him from the bottom of her heart.

"No." Emmy grabbed his hand. "I want my daddy."

Daddy? The last time he'd heard "Da-Da" had been from Emma's mouth, and she'd been just under a year old. Now to hear the word *Daddy* on Emmy's lips thrilled him to his core.

Pamela placed her hands on her hips. "That's enough." She pointed down the hall. "Both of you go to your room so I can talk with Jack."

"But—" the girls said in unison.

"No buts. Go."

Emma raced to the bedroom, but Emmy grabbed him in a quick hug. Overwhelmed with thanksgiving that he had one ally in the house, Jack roped his arms around her and, ignoring the strong mayonnaise odor, kissed her forehead.

"I'm glad you're here, Daddy."

"Me, too."

He released her, and she raced to the bedroom to join her sister. He stood up and gazed at Pamela. "I can't believe she's taken to me so quickly."

Pamela folded her arms in front of her chest. "She's always been like that. Bubbly. Outgoing. Ready to give anyone a chance. Forgiving."

Jack touched his wife's arm. "I hope someday you'll be able to forgive me."

She stepped back. "It's not that easy, Jack." Unfolding

her arms, she pointed down the hall. "You saw Emma. Not everyone can just pretend that eight years apart was nothing."

He wanted to nestle Emma close, promise her that he'd never leave her again, that she could count on him to be the daddy she'd deserved from the beginning.

Pamela closed her eyes and wiped her hand down her face. "I shouldn't have called you. I hadn't prepared the girls. I was—"

Jack covered the space between them and wrapped his arms around Pamela. She didn't move and, for a moment, he held his breath, waiting for her to push him away. Instead, she leaned closer. Her arms remained planted at her sides, but she allowed his embrace. "Thank you for calling me, Pamela."

She pulled away, and he felt the emptiness in his arms all the way to his toes. "You better go home."

"Let me vacuum the furniture and the floors first. You still have to put mayonnaise in Emma's hair."

She shook her head, but Jack continued. "And wash the gunk out of their hair and put the sheets back on the beds. The least I can do is vacuum."

She worried the inside of her mouth, then finally consented. "Okay."

Jack vacuumed the furniture and the floor then cleaned the vacuum filter. He took out the trash. While Pamela put the sheets back on the beds, he cleaned the dishes. By the time he'd finished, he heard the three of them in the girls' room saying prayers. He smiled when Emmy thanked God for bringing him back into their lives.

When Pamela walked out of the bedroom, Jack picked

up his keys from the counter. "I'll come over and vac-uum for you tomorrow, if you'd like."

"We'll see." She shifted her weight from one foot to the other. "If you'd like to come to the festival, we'll be at the school at six."

Jack couldn't stop his grin. "You mean it?"

Pamela didn't look at him, only nodded.

"I'll be there." Before she could protest, he leaned over and placed a quick kiss on the top of her head. He walked to the front door then stopped. "I love you, Pammer."

Pammer. The nickname Jack had given her when they were high school sweethearts rolled around in her mind for two days. His declaration of love, the sincerity in his gaze before he'd walked out the door, the kiss on her forehead, the warmth and strength of his embrace. They all haunted her.

Emma grabbed Pamela's hand and pulled her toward the door. "Come on, Mom. Kirk and Callie are already at Grandma and Grandpa's."

Peeking out the window, Pamela saw her brother and sister-in-law cross the yard and walk in the back door of the B and B. She couldn't deny that living a yard length behind her parents and a few yard lengths away from her brother and sister-in-law did have its advantages. Gath-ering together for family dinner nights was literally a hop, skip and a jump away from the cabin.

Pamela shooed her girls toward the front door. "Well, go on over there." She snapped her fingers. "Emma, grab the dinner rolls off the kitchen table first."

The girls raced out the door, and Pamela opened the oven door and lifted out the apple crisps. Part of her wanted to place one on a dish to save for Jack, maybe take it to him as a thank-you for helping with the girls and the house. She shook her head. She didn't want to encourage him and didn't have the strength to give him the opportunity to break her heart again.

Besides, now she had the girls to think about. They would feel the pain of his addiction and the hurt of his abandonment as deeply as she, and she simply would not put them at risk.

Gently, she placed each hot apple crisp on a plate. She made the dessert every October, and yet today as she'd cut apples, she'd thought of Jack and how much he loved them. While she combined sugar, flour and cinnamon, she envisioned him closing his eyes, rubbing his belly and oohing and aahing over the dessert. When she dropped the oat mixture on top of the apples and then put the pan in the oven, she remembered him taking her in his arms and sweeping kisses on her mouth, cheeks, nose and forehead in thanks for making his favorite.

As she placed the last of the crisps on the plate, her cheeks burned with the memory of those kisses and his touch. She couldn't deny she missed him. For years, she'd squelched passion, a need for touch, a desire for warmth, but seeing him again had brought all those needs and feelings back. They made her light-headed and vulnerable.

Leaning forward, she placed her elbows on the counter and dropped her head into her hands. Why had she told him he could come to the festival? She didn't want to be around him. Didn't want to feel weak in his presence, like she'd lost every ounce of good sense. She didn't need to be vulnerable.

Standing up straight, she scooped the plate off the

counter. *Feel. Need. Want.* All words of a woman who didn't have a backbone. And one thing Jack's leaving had given her was a strong spine. Ignoring her emotions, she determined to focus on her mind. On her good sense. She wouldn't allow herself to be swayed by charm, memories or even the promise of his having changed.

She walked across the yard to her parents' house. She put the dish on the counter, then joined the family in the living area. Emmy sat cuddled up beside Callie, her hand resting on Callie's ever-so-slightly swollen belly. Kirk sat beside them on the couch, his arm behind his wife's shoulders. Mom and Emma shared the wingback chair, and Dad sat in the leather recliner.

"Why can't I feel them yet?" asked Emmy.

"They're still too little." Kirk lifted his hand and curled his finger and thumb about an inch and a half apart. "Only as big as a fig, so their kicks aren't very strong yet."

"But you said you heard their heartbeats," said Emmy.

Callie looked over at Pamela and smiled. Pink cheeks, bright eyes, shiny blond hair that touched her shoulders. She really did glow with sheer maternal happiness. "We heard their heartbeats today at the doctor's visit."

Pamela wanted to be excited for her brother and Callie. And she couldn't wait to meet her twin nieces or nephews. She looked at her brother, his chin and chest lifted in pride, and jealousy niggled at her gut. She'd never seen that in Jack. He'd been shocked and less than thrilled when they'd discovered their first unplanned pregnancy. The second sent Jack over the edge. His aloofness had ripped away part of her joy at becoming a new mother. Pushing away her selfish feelings, she smiled at her sister-in-law. "That's wonderful. They're getting bigger every day."

Emmy placed her mouth against Callie's belly. "Yes, you are. Now, hurry up and grow so I can feel you kick."

The family laughed, and Emmy sat up, her cheeks and neck pink.

"So, what's this I hear about Jack going to the fall festival tomorrow?" her dad asked.

"I don't want him to go," said Emma as she crossed her arms in front of her chest.

Pamela's mother draped her arm around Emma's shoulders. "You don't? Why not?"

Emma lowered her gaze and stuck out her lip. "He left us."

Kirk leaned forward on the couch and placed his elbows on his knees. "He did leave, and he was wrong, but he's sorry, and he loves God now and wants to get to know you girls."

Pamela's jaw dropped. If anyone else in the family would be opposed to her estranged husband trying to walk back into their lives, she'd assumed it would be Kirk. "You've talked with Jack?"

Kirk looked up at her and nodded. "He came by the farm last week. Helped me feed the animals and clean up the petting zoo and activity center. We talked a long while."

Pamela clamped her lips together as anger bubbled in her stomach and rose into her chest. How dare Jack talk to her brother behind her back! He could do and say whatever he wanted to weasel his way back into the family, but they didn't know him as she did. They didn't know the times she'd hidden his drunkenness from them.

"I'm glad," said Emmy. "He's going to take me to

play the games and do the cake walk and jump on the bouncy things."

Pamela looked at her older daughter. Bitterness and anger marred Emma's expression, and Pamela's heart twisted with pain. *God, what has happened to my sweet girl?*

She blinked at the quick prayer. What would God do to help Emma? Nothing. Maybe it was good for Emma to learn at a young age that life was hard and the world was cruel. She glanced at her younger daughter, who twirled a strand of long hair between her fingers and continued to pat Callie's stomach. Kirk and Callie stared at each other as if nothing in the world could shake them. *Or maybe it's time I tried trusting God again.*

"Give him a chance."

Pamela turned to see her mother talking into Emma's ear. She kissed her granddaughter's cheek, and Emma rested her head on her grandma's shoulder. Hurt still traced Emma's features, and Pamela bit back the tears that threatened to spill down her cheeks.

Give him a chance. Give him a chance. Her family's advice washed over her like a hot shower on a cold day. But sometimes the water was too hot, and the steam took away all ability to breathe. Gasping at the pressure against her chest, Pamela turned and walked away from her family.

She had to be strong. Jack had the ability to rip her heart into shreds. Again. She couldn't take that chance.

Chapter 8

Pamela placed the orange-and-black bracelet on the plastic hook of the fishing pole, then tugged the line. The small girl on the other side of the wooden partition that was decorated with an ocean theme lifted the hook over and squealed when she saw her prize. Emma pulled her sweater sleeve, and Pamela looked at her daughter. She pointed to the plastic spider she'd just stuck on the hook. "Gabe will love this."

Peeking around the partition, Pamela spied a dark-haired boy who'd been in Emma's class since kindergarten. She'd wondered if her daughter had a crush on the little urchin. Judging by the blossoms of pink on each of Emma's cheeks, Pamela's assumption had been correct.

She grinned at her girl. Emma looked adorable with her long hair French braided with a dark brown bow wrapped around the bottom of the mane. The green-

and-brown polka-dotted shirt complimented the brown corduroy skirt and brown boots with fur at the top. She and the girls had enjoyed buying a few new outfits with the money she'd gotten from Jack.

Emma's friend, Sabrina, raced up to the makeshift booth, and they hugged. Sabrina tugged at Emma's shirt. "Come on. Let's go play."

Emma frowned. "I'm helping my mom."

Pamela waved to Sabrina's parents, who stood beside the beanbag-tossing game. "I'll be fine. Go play."

Emma's face lit up, and Pamela realized it had been a while since she'd seen her daughter smile so big. "Really?"

"Of course." She shooed her away. "Go on."

Pamela placed another trinket on the plastic hook, then sat on the stool. With the start of the cake walk, fewer children came to the booth.

"You need some help?"

Pamela gasped when she looked up at her former professor. "Peter, what are you doing here?"

"It's been a few days since I've seen you. I knew your girls came to this school." He shrugged. "So, here I am."

Pamela thought of the past few days. She'd washed sheets, vacuumed and checked both girls' hair for nits each day. Just to be sure she'd conquered the little critters, she planned to smother their hair in mayonnaise again over the weekend. She thought of Jack and his willingness to dig right in and help. She couldn't imagine Peter being so willing. And she still didn't know why Jack had known so much about delousing a person and a house.

Pushing her thoughts away, she patted the stool beside her. "Have a seat. As you can tell, I'm not busy at the moment."

He sat beside her, then placed his hand on the top of her knee. "So, what have you been up to these last few days?"

Pamela stiffened. Uncomfortable, she pivoted, allowing his hand to fall off her leg. "Nothing much. Studying and cleaning."

Both true statements, although she had no intention of expounding on how much cleaning had been involved. The smell of his musky cologne wafted to her nostrils, and she sucked in a deep breath. He smelled delicious, as always. His hair lay in perfect dark waves, and his light eyes reminded her of ocean waves splashing against the shore. And yet, she'd felt squeamish when he'd touched her leg.

"Hi, Mommy."

Pamela turned, and warmth traveled up her neck and cheeks at the sight of Emmy with Jack beside her. His brows formed a single line above confused eyes. She cleared her throat. "Are you having fun?"

Emmy handed her a tray of six cupcakes decorated with pumpkins. "See what Daddy and I won at the cake walk."

Pamela glanced at Peter, noting the surprise on his face. She cleared her throat again and pointed to Jack. "Peter, this is Jack. He's—"

"Her husband." Jack extended his hand. "And you are?"

Peter lifted his chin. "Peter Dane. A friend of Pamela's."

Looking from one man to the other, Pamela noted the set jaws, the piercing gazes. If she didn't know better, she might expect one of them to ask the other to step outside to exchange blows.

Exhaling a long breath, Pamela peered at Jack. "Actually, Jack is legally my husband, but he hasn't been part of my life for the past eight years."

Jack's gaze stayed focused on Peter as he crossed his arms in front of his chest. "That's going to change."

Pamela bit back a growl. "And Peter was my professor two semesters ago."

"Yes, and now—"

Pamela lifted her hand and cut him off. "Emmy, what are you and your dad planning to do now?"

She giggled. "We're going to play on the bouncy things."

Pamela stared up at Jack. "That sounds like a great idea." Pamela pushed his arm. "Take Emmy to the inflatables. You can meet me back here in an hour."

Jack opened his mouth, then clamped it shut. With a quick nod, he grabbed Emmy's hand, turned and walked out of the school's gymnasium.

"You're still married?"

Irritation laced through Peter's words, and Pamela shifted toward him and looked him in the eye. "I am."

"But?"

"He's been gone for eight years. This month he showed up wanting to start over."

"And what do you want?"

"I want nothing to do with him."

Peter's eyes lit up as he smiled. "Terrific."

Just because she didn't want anything to do with Jack didn't mean she wanted to start something with Peter. If the past few minutes were a preview to what life would be like with a man in her life again, then she'd pass.

She hadn't needed a man for a long time, and she most certainly wasn't about to start yearning for one now if it meant tension thicker than her financial planning textbook. Peter seemed to be a nice guy. She'd enjoyed him as a teacher, and there was no denying the guy was easy on the eyes, but her girls came first.

Biting her bottom lip, she placed a trinket on the plastic hook for the little boy who'd just given Peter a ticket. Life had been so much easier a month ago. No Jack. No Peter. Just school and her girls.

And your anger and bitterness.

Pamela blinked. Where had that come from? She remembered the sadness on Emma's face the night before at her parents' house. Surely Emma hadn't gotten those feelings from her.

Jack and Pamela stood behind Emma and Emmy at the counter of the ice-cream parlor. The mom-and-pop place had the same fifties decor he'd enjoyed when he was a child, though the owners had added a few pieces, refurbished the booths and repainted the walls. It had been one of his favorite places to take Pamela when they'd dated, and now it felt right to take his daughters, as well. He sneaked a peek at Pamela and wondered if she shared his nostalgic memories.

Once Emma and Emmy placed orders for a peanut butter shake with chocolate candies and a fudge milkshake with whipped cream, Jack turned to his wife. "Hot fudge sundae, no nuts, extra whipped cream and an extra cherry?"

She nodded slowly and he ordered one for both of them. She studied him as he paid for the snack. Everything in him wanted to turn to her, grab her by the shoulders and proclaim that he knew everything about her, remembered the good, the bad and all the in-between. Alcohol had imprisoned him behind a lock only God could break through, but he'd never stopped paying attention, never stopped loving her.

Taking their treats to a booth, Emma grabbed her mother's hand and nudged her to sit beside her. While Emmy talked about colliding with a friend on the inflatable, Jack studied his older daughter, wondering what he could do to get her to trust him.

It's gonna take time. Jermaine's words from last week's phone call rang through his mind. *Time and consistency. You're gonna have to prove to that girl you ain't leavin' her again.*

Jack took a bite of his sundae. He'd learned a great deal about patience in the years it took to get back on track. Meditating on God's word, going to school, working at the shelter and staying sober had taught him about learning to wait. But since moving back to Tennessee, Jack found himself anxious to get started with life, to take Pamela back in his arms, to love and care for his girls.

"Hi, Pamela, Emma, Emmy."

Jack blinked away his thoughts and looked up at the family standing beside the booth. Emma sat up straight.

Pamela smiled as she pointed to Jack. "Wayne, Libby, this is…" She paused.

Emmy wrapped her hands around his arm. "It's our daddy, Jack."

Questions covered the couple's features, and Jack found himself biting back frustration.

Emma grinned at the girl beside Wayne and Libby. "Sabrina, I didn't know you were coming here."

The blond-haired girl giggled. "I didn't know you were gonna be here, either."

"Mom, can I go sit with Sabrina?"

"Well…" Pamela pursed her lips.

"It's fine with us." Libby glanced from Pamela to him, then placed her hand on her chin. "I mean, if it's okay with you."

Jack clasped his hands, wanting nothing more than for the couple to leave the side of the booth. This was an additional point he hadn't considered when he'd returned to Bloom Hollow—the people who didn't know him and had no clue that his wife and daughters did indeed have a husband and dad. "I think it will be fine. Don't you, hon?"

She narrowed her eyes, and Jack realized the endearment had slipped from his lips. It was no secret that he wanted to renew their relationship, but she'd also made it clear she wasn't ready. Part of him didn't mind the fire that lit those eyes. The fire was better than emptiness. He still stirred her emotions. He'd just have to work on which ones.

Pamela nudged Emma. "You can sit with them."

Emma jumped up, and she and Sabrina raced to a booth across the parlor. Emmy tugged his sleeve. "Daddy, will you let me out? I gotta go to the bathroom."

Pamela opened her mouth, and Emmy lifted her hands. "I know. I know. I'll wash my hands."

Jack grinned at Emmy's emphatic tone. She sounded much older than her eight years. After letting her out, he sat back down. "You don't have to go with her?"

She motioned around the shop. "We're in a small-town ice-cream parlor. She's eight years old. She'll be fine." She took a bite of her sundae, then shoved the spoon into the cup. "Besides, we need to talk."

Jack wiped his face. "Yes, we do."

"Don't call me 'hon.'"

"But I love you."

Pamela narrowed her gaze again. "Doesn't matter. Don't do it."

"Fine." He put his elbows on the table and leaned closer to her. "I want to see you and the girls every day."

She snorted. "I don't think so."

He'd known what her response would be, but he wanted her to hear what he desired, what he hoped for, what he prayed nightly for. Since seeing that Peter character sitting on the stool beside her, Jack determined that he would let her know each time he saw her that he intended to win her back.

"I want to set up times to see you."

"To see the girls."

"And you."

"Just the girls."

"Do you really think Emma is ready to see me without you?"

The question tasted bitter coming from his lips. It hurt, but the words were true. Emma wasn't ready to spend time with him without her mother.

Pamela wrinkled her nose. "You're right. But it doesn't always have to be me. It could be Mom or Dad or Kirk." She crossed her arms. "And you already know they're all ready and willing to welcome you back into our lives."

Jack grinned. He couldn't help it. It thrilled him that her family wanted to give him a second chance. "I'm going to win you back, Pammer."

"This isn't a game to win, Jack. The finish line doesn't happen until you're dead. Family life is the journey, and you have to be present to participate."

"You're right, and I want to take every next step with you. Please forgive me."

Pamela didn't respond, simply twirled her spoon in the sundae. "When do you want to see them again?"

"Tomorrow."

She shook her head. "No."

"When?"

Pamela sighed as she jabbed the spoon into the sundae. "Sunday. After church."

Two days! He'd expected her to say a week or more. Figured he'd have to argue for a sooner date, but two days was perfect.

"Okay." Jack reached into his pocket and handed her a check. "To help with bills and such."

She nodded as she placed the money in her purse. "I think I'll go check on Emmy."

Jack watched her walk away. She'd agreed to let him see the girls again and she'd taken the money without a fight. They were making progress.

Chapter 9

Pamela placed two cans of green beans in the grocery cart, then waited while her mom stocked up on canned vegetables and set them in her own cart.

Callie rested her hand against her belly. "I'm finally feeling less nauseated, but my stomach still cramps something fierce."

"Just your uterus expanding," Tammie said.

Callie nodded. "That's what the doctor said, but it's kinda scary." She grabbed a can of sauerkraut and placed it in the cart, then shrugged. "Been craving cabbage."

Pamela marked off green beans from the grocery list. "I remember that and feeling like there had to be something wrong."

Callie pointed to her chest. "But I'm a nurse. I knew cramps were to be expected. Just never dreamed they would hurt so much."

Mom patted Callie's shoulder. "You'll likely feel even more discomfort with two babies."

"Yep. She told me that, too." Callie clasped her hands together. "But I'm okay with the cramping, as long as everything is all right." She lifted her shoulders. "I still can't believe Kirk and I got pregnant so easily. I just figured…"

Mom cupped Callie's chin. "God is so good."

Pamela didn't wait for her sister-in-law and mother. She pushed her cart ahead to the next aisle. Grabbing a couple of boxes of cereal and oatmeal from the shelf, she tried to flush the morning sermon and her mom's words from her mind.

Everyone wanted to talk about God's goodness. Sure, He got the Israelites across the river on dry land. Yes, He'd shut the lions' mouth and kept the Hebrew boys from burning in Nebuchadnezzar's fire. And he'd brought Callie back to Bloom Hollow, allowed her and Kirk to fall in love again, healed her from cancer and even let her get pregnant.

But He seemed to pick and choose the people to show His goodness to. And some got the shaft. Like Moses. He led the Israelites out of Egypt, got mad at them, rightfully so, and hit a rock, and then God told him he couldn't see the Promised Land. Or Stephen, a man who'd pledged his life to Jesus, helped the Greek widows, stood up for his belief in Christ and was stoned to death. *And look at me. I thought I was following You, Lord. I wanted to be a good wife and mother. It was all I wanted. Then Jack…*

"We'd better hurry." Her mom's words broke into her reverie. "It's almost time to close the activity center and petting zoo, and I want to say goodbye to Ben before he heads back to the university."

"Yeah, and I don't know what time Jack is bringing the girls back. I still can't believe Emma went with him."

"I think she was really excited to see that new movie," said Callie.

Pamela rushed through the rest of the shopping. Within moments, they'd paid for their purchases, loaded the SUV and headed back to the farm. By the time they'd unpacked all the groceries, Dad, Kirk and Ben were heading toward the B and B.

"Vegetable soup is on the stove and ready," said her mom. "Wash up."

"Sounds good," Mike said as he wiped his forehead with the back of his hand.

"Busy today?" asked Callie as Kirk wrapped his arms around her and kissed her.

Pamela's cheeks warmed. She'd thought and dreamed more about hugs and kisses the past few weeks than she had in eight years, and seeing her brother's and Callie's expressions of love and happiness sent shivers of longing through her.

Kirk released his wife, then tapped her nose. "Very." He laid his hand on her stomach. "How are my boys doing?"

"Boys!" Pamela crowed. "You just might have you a set of girls."

"Nah." Kirk took Callie's hand in his. "They're boys."

"We'll see," Callie crooned as they walked hand in hand into the house.

Pamela lifted her chin and gazed up at Ben. The boy had grown to be every bit of six foot three inches, if not taller. Dark hair and light eyes, he looked a lot like Kirk, only thinner. "How are you, little brother?"

"Doing all right. Busy."

"How's school?"

He wrinkled his nose. "It's going."

"I have a financial class that's giving me fits."

Ben huffed. "Wish there was only one class driving me nuts."

Pamela had been worried about Ben. He seemed pre-occupied each time he visited, and he often sported dark circles beneath his eyes. "But you've always been so good at school."

He made a fist and lightly punched her shoulder. "Still am. No worrying about me, big sister."

They turned at the sound of car tires crunching against the gravel driveway. Jack stopped the car, and the girls jumped out of the backseat. "Uncle Ben!"

Ben scowled at Pamela. "What is he doing here?"

Pamela raised her eyebrows. "You didn't know he'd come back? I just figured Mom and Dad told you—"

"You let him come back?"

The girls reached Ben, and he bent down and gave them hugs and kisses on the foreheads. "Grandma's got soup ready. Why don't you go make me a bowl?"

"Okay!" said Emmy.

"No, I'm going to do it!" said Emma.

"No, me!"

Ben stalked toward Jack's car, his hands knotted into fists. Pamela gripped his arm. "No, Ben."

He stopped and glared at her. "What are you thinking? Don't you remember how upset you were? And the girls?"

Pamela stomped her foot. "Of course I remember."

"Then have you lost your sense? I thought you were smarter than this."

Pamela curled her lip. "How dare you? You have no idea what I've been going through. I didn't ask him to come back. I'm terrified he'll ruin it all, start drinking and leave again, then I'll be left with the mess to clean up." Emotion choked her throat, and tears stung her eyes.

Jack stood beside them. Pamela hadn't heard him get out of the car. Her stomach churned, and heat warmed her cheeks. He raised his hands when Ben pivoted toward him and raised his fist.

"I won't fight you, Ben."

"That doesn't surprise me." Ben spat the words. "You were a coward then, and you're still a coward."

Jack kept his hands raised. "I've given my life to God. I've changed and—"

"God!" Ben huffed and a string of curses slipped from his lips.

"Ben?" Pamela gawked at her brother. She'd never heard him talk that way, never seen him so angry.

His eyes glazed with loathing and pain that went deeper than any feeling he could have for Jack. His jaw set into a firm line as he shoved his hands into his pockets. "What do I care anyway? I'll eat me a little soup, then I'm out of here."

Stunned, she watched as her brother stormed toward the house. She glanced at Jack, still trying to make sense of what had happened. "I'm sorry. I don't know what came over…"

She couldn't finish. Anger and bitterness had warred for victory in her life the past few years, and sometimes won battles, but Ben's countenance and words had been dark and devastating. Despair punched her gut, and she prayed her heart hadn't grown so cold. She didn't understand why God allowed hardship, and yet she missed laying her burdens at His feet.

"It's okay. He has the right to be mad at me."

"I know, but…" She stopped again. As many times as she had failed, God had the right to be mad at her, as well, and yet she couldn't deny a continuous urge within her to cry out for His comfort.

Jack clasped his hands in front of him. "I had a great time with the girls, Pammer." He shifted his weight, then unclasped his hands. "I love them. And I love you."

He turned on his heels and got back in his car and drove off. Tears welled in Pamela's eyes. Why couldn't life be simpler?

Jack put the last of the sliced ham and a piece of cheese on the bun, then wrapped the sandwich in cellophane. In an hour, he and some of the leaders of Faith Church would officially open The Refuge's doors. He'd sent pictures of the inside and outside of the building to Jermaine and Stella and to his parents, Kari and Todd via email and couldn't wait to tell them how the first day went.

"Jack, will you join us in the office for a minute?" Pastor Mark called from another room.

"Sure." Jack set the tray of sandwiches in the refrigerator. His heart swelled as he looked at the bottles of water, juice boxes, veggie cups and fruit cups lining the shelves inside. He was ready to serve, and once again he silently petitioned the Lord to use him to make a difference in someone's life.

After washing his hands, he joined the pastor and three of the church's deacons in the office. Teresa and another woman he didn't recognize were also there. He offered a grin in Teresa's direction, but she averted her gaze. Just as well. At least she wasn't showing up alone every day.

Mark patted his back. "Jack, you've done a great job overseeing this ministry. We're thankful you chose to come to The Refuge to serve the Lord."

The men mumbled their agreement, and warmth traipsed up his neck. He didn't do it for their pats on the back. He did it because the Lord had saved him from alcoholism and homelessness. How could he not serve his God?

Pastor Mark pointed to the front door. "Before we officially open, I'd like to take a moment to praise God for giving us this opportunity and to ask His blessing to reach the lost." He took Jack's hand and the man's beside him. "Jack, if you'll start the prayer, we'll go around the circle and I'll finish up."

Jack praised God for deliverance and prayed for guidance, strength and wisdom in directing the shelter. As the others voiced their prayers, Jack's spirit settled into a peace that transcended all understanding. God would provide for the shelter. He would provide food, clothes, bedding, all the material items they'd need. He'd provide workers, ready to serve. And he'd provide the homeless, who desperately needed salvation as well as a warm meal and a place to rest their heads.

With a pride only God could give, Jack walked out of the office and opened the front door. Within the hour, a long-haired man with an unkempt beard wandered inside. The layers of clothes he wore were filthy. The jacket had a wet spot covering his left elbow. It had been a while since Jack had experienced the stench of someone who couldn't tell you when he'd last bathed. Smelling it now brought back the memories.

Jack extended his hand. "Welcome to The Refuge."

The man cocked his head, and Jack could tell by the faraway look in his eyes that he suffered from a mental illness or drugs had taken his mental health. Still, he took Jack's hand in his dirty, calloused one. "Morning, Steve."

"I'm Jack. I'm glad you're here. Let's get you some lunch."

"Jack, you say?" The man cocked his head to the other side. "You look just like my brother, Steve."

"Nope. I'm Jack. What's your name?"

The man scratched his beard. "Well, wait a minute." He laughed, exposing half-rotten teeth, and smacked his hand against his leg. "I'm Steve." The man sniffed. "You say you got some hamburgers?"

Jack shook his head. "No. But we have ham sandwiches. Would you like one?"

Steve shrugged. "I suppose." He clutched the bag he carried to his chest. "You don't mind if I take my stuff with me."

"Not at all. Do you mind to show me what you have?"

Steve squinted. "Why? You gonna steal somethin'?"

Jack shook his head. "No, but I need to make sure everything in there is safe for all of us."

He recalled the time at God's Hands that a man had pulled a knife on another guy because he had taken the man's regular seat at one of the tables. After that, he or Jermaine had to check bags before allowing anyone to eat or sleep at the shelter. Some of the homeless refused to stay because they feared his and Jermaine's motives were to harm them. It pained Jack to turn people away.

He knew the things in their bags were materially all they had in the world, but he also had to keep the workers and other homeless guests safe.

Steve worried the inside of his mouth for several moments. With a shake of his head, he dumped the contents of the bag on the table. "I suppose I'm hungry enough to let you have a little peek."

With no weapons to be found, Jack told him he could put the stuff back in the bag, then showed him where to find the food. Teresa seemed a bit shaky as she handed him a tray of food, but when Steve passed her, she smiled fully, lighting up her whole face.

Before long five more men showed up, and, after checking to see they were safe, he guided them to the kitchen area. When time came to close the doors for the night, three of the six men opted to stay.

After locking up, Jack settled into the office with a Bible and notebook. He wrote about all that happened that day, then spent time in God's word. Normally he wouldn't spend the night, as the church had hired workers to stay. But tonight he couldn't help it, as thanksgiving at God's mercy and grace overwhelmed him.

Before he closed the Bible and journal, he scribbled one more petition.

I don't deserve it, Lord, but please restore my marriage.

Chapter 10

Pamela zipped up her sweater. Dr. Mays's classroom was freezing, as usual. She knew he had nothing to do with the temperature of the room, because half the building was frigid and the other half hot as a sauna. Still, the coolness coupled with his incessant droning made her want to cuddle up in a blanket and take a nap.

Sneaking her phone from her purse, she scanned the recent text messages. She'd sent multiple texts to Ben after he'd stormed away from her and Jack a month ago, but he wouldn't respond. He wouldn't take her calls, either. Something was going on with Ben. He'd become distant, unhappy, tired. *At least he still takes Mom's calls. I know he hasn't fallen off the face of the planet.*

She turned off the phone and stared up at her professor. Her grade would most likely be higher if she paid attention. But listening to him was like balancing a checkbook without knowing the numbers. Thankfully, she had strong As in her other classes. After refiguring her grade point average, she learned she could get a C in this class and keep her scholarship. She tapped her pencil against her cheek. *I can't believe I'm willing to get a C.* She huffed. Who was she kidding? She prayed her grade would be that high.

"I finished grading your papers," said Dr. Mays.

Pamela sat up straighter. He was the only professor she had who didn't accept electronic submissions, which only went to show how long the man had been teaching and that it was past time for retirement. Her other professors wouldn't accept paper copies.

"You're free to go once you receive your score."

Pamela waited as he shuffled up one aisle and down the other. Her feet twitched, and she clasped and unclasped her hands. Her paper must be the last one in his stack. Finally, he stopped beside her and placed the paper on her desk. She stared at the bold red letter. B.

Releasing a deep breath, she scooped up the work and shoved it in her bag. *Thank you, God.*

She didn't even shake off the praise. It seemed to slip from her lips and mind all the time, and she'd almost given up fighting it. For a month Jack had been true to his word. He took the girls each time she allowed him, even came to dinner whenever Mom and Dad invited him. Each week he gave her a check to help with expenses. She felt confident he kept very little of his income for himself. Though she hadn't given over to the feelings, she couldn't deny the fast beating of her heart when he was near.

"Pamela."

She stopped and closed her eyes at the sound of Peter's voice. She'd tried to avoid him since that night at the fall festival.

"It seems like it's been forever since I've seen you," he said as he stopped beside her.

Pamela nodded. "Yes. I've been busy."

"With Jack."

She frowned. It wasn't his business if she had been busy because of Jack. She and Peter hadn't gone on a date, didn't have any kind of relationship. He'd expressed interest and taken her to a mechanic and that was it.

He shifted his feet. "I mean—"

"Actually, I've been busy trying to keep my grade up in Dr. Mays's class and with my girls. And, yes, with Jack."

"But I thought that maybe—"

Pamela lifted her hand. "Listen, Peter. I'm sorry, but I'm not going to be able to go out with you. I appreciate the offer, but—"

"Do you really think he's better for you? He left."

Pamela stared at the man she barely knew. "How would you know that?" She motioned from him to herself. "You don't know me. You don't know anything about my life."

"I know you lack wisdom in discerning good character."

As she took in his clean, stiff shirt and neatly pressed pants, she could tell he cared about appearances. His light eyes, which she'd once likened to ocean waves, now seemed empty of compassion. He hadn't called her, hadn't tried to contact her in a month. And if she remembered correctly, he didn't speak a word to her girls at the festival. She hefted her bag onto her shoulder. "Actually, I think I'm a pretty good judge of character. Bye, Peter."

She turned away from him and stomped to her car. The man had some nerve! *At least I didn't go out with him. Yet another thing to be thankful for.*

Jack twirled around on the ice skates, then took Emmy's hands in his. "Just relax, and I'll guide you until you get the feel of those skates."

Emmy's eyes widened with uncertainty, but a full smile still lifted her lips. "Okay, Daddy."

His heart still flipped each time his younger daughter called him that, each time he saw faith in him gleaming in her eyes. He'd done nothing to deserve an ally, but God had blessed him with one anyway, and Jack believed with every fiber of his being that their family would be restored one day.

Emmy's left foot slipped. She gasped, and he gripped her hands tighter and held her upright. "I've got you. Just allow one foot to kinda glide in front of the o. .er."

"Like walking with a swoosh."

He chuckled at her analogy. Spying Emma and Pamela clinging to the ice-skating center's wall, he prayed they would have a good time. He remembered the last time he and Pamela had ice-skated together, the winter of their senior year of high school. Only a few months before they'd married.

She'd held on to him, just as Emmy did now. Love and trust had gleamed in her eyes, the same way it did now in his younger daughter's. Holding Pamela tight, guiding her across the ice, he'd felt as if he could conquer the world. He would have never imagined that in a year's time she'd be his wife, carrying his first child, and that the bottle would take over as primary love of his life.

"I think I can do it on my own, Daddy."

Jack smiled at his child. A long strand of red hair fell into her eyes, and she brushed it away. "You sure?"

She bit her bottom lip and nodded. He let her go, and she wobbled a moment, then straightened herself and skated on her own. She giggled. "I'm doing it."

"You're doing great." He pointed toward the wall. "How 'bout I go see if Emma will let me help her?"

"Okay."

Jack skated to Emma. Frustration marked her features as she clung to the bar on the wall.

Pamela held on only a few feet behind her. She chortled. "I'm afraid I'm not very good at this."

"I remember."

Pamela jutted out her chin and looked up at him. He winked at her, and her expression softened. Her voice carried a hint of teasing as she said, "Of all the places to take the girls. Ice-skating?"

He shrugged. "Emmy begged me. I couldn't say no."

Pamela clicked her tongue. "She's definitely your kid."

His heart pounded with a thrill, and he swallowed back the knot in his throat. He nodded toward their older daughter. "And it appears Emma is yours." He extended his hands to her. "You wanna let me help you? I'll hold your hands. Won't let you fall."

Emma glanced back at her mom.

Pamela nodded toward the center. "Go ahead, Emma. Let him take you. You'll have fun."

Emma's voice sounded like a squeak. "I'll fall."

Pamela shook her head. "He won't let you. He never let me fall."

His gaze locked with hers at the words. He'd held her tight all the years of dating in high school and the first several months of marriage. Then he'd let her down. Let her fall. Hard.

God, I don't deserve her forgiveness.

Scriptures about trusting God came to mind.

Trusting the words of his spirit, he lifted his eyebrows and extended his hands to Emma. To his surprise, she grabbed hold. He guided her onto the ice. She didn't look up at him; she focused on her feet instead. He encouraged her to allow the skates to glide across the ice, but she remained stiff and wouldn't look up.

"Look at me, Emma." Emmy waved as she skated tentatively past them.

Emma looked up for a brief moment, wobbled and then grabbed his hands tighter.

"Don't worry—I've got you."

A voice boomed over the speakers. "Ladies and gentlemen, boys and girls, it's Zamboni time."

Emma looked up at him questioningly. "What's that?"

"They're going to clean the ice." He guided her toward the exit. "Let's get some nachos and slushes."

She smiled, and Jack's heart melted. "Okay."

Emmy skated beside him. "Daddy, what are we doing?"

"They've got to clean the ice," said Emma in her big-sister voice. "But we're gonna get some nachos and slushes."

Emmy clapped her hands. "Yay!"

After taking off their skates, they walked to the concession and ordered a snack. Once at a table, the girls chattered back and forth about wobbles and near falls while trying to move around the ice. Each story sounded scarier than the one before, and yet neither of the girls had fallen a single time.

Jack watched Pamela as she listened to the girls' tales. She was a good mom, and he hoped one day she would share some of the things he'd missed. Like Emmy's birth. Was it easier than Emma's? When did she start walking? Did the girls fight when they were smaller? Now they seemed to be good friends. Different as night and day, but buddies just the same. What were their first words? What were their first days of school like? He'd missed so much. Had they asked about him? Did they know about the night he left? "Thanks for your patience." The same voice sounded over the speaker. "Let's start the new hour with a couples' skate."

Emma looked at Pamela and pointed toward him. "Are you gonna skate with Daddy?"

Pamela started to shake her head no, but Emmy bounced in her seat and clapped her hands. "Yeah, Mommy, do it. Daddy's a great skater. He won't let you fall."

Jack lifted his brows and held out his hand. "She's right."

At first he'd believed she would say no, but instead she bent down and put on her skates. Jack's heart raced in his chest as he laced up his own.

Taking her hand in his, he guided her onto the ice. In one quick motion, he twirled around to skate backward, then gripped her hands tight. She gasped when she lost her balance for a moment. "Jack, you said you wouldn't let me fall."

He peered into her eyes. "With God's help, I'll never let you fall again."

Pamela looked away from him, and he knew she'd heard his words exactly as he'd meant them.

"I love you, Pamela."

She stared up at him. "Can we just skate without all the heavy?"

"Absolutely."

He held her hands, relishing their softness, longing for the touches he'd once known, but he didn't say anything else. He remembered. He enjoyed. And he prayed for a second chance at her love.

The song ended, and the girls joined them on the rink. Emmy grew more confident skating, and Emma softened toward him. He watched and relished when Pamela laughed with the girls, tucking away each moment deep into his heart.

Once the day ended, he drove them back to the cabin. He walked them to the door, and Emmy wrapped her arms around his waist. "Thanks, Daddy. I had a bunch of fun."

She scampered into the house. To his surprise, Emma gave him a tentative hug. He wrapped his arms around her. "Thanks, Dad," she whispered, then raced into the house.

His gut twisted, and tears welled in his eyes. He blinked them away as he looked at Pamela. She smiled. "It was a lot of fun. Night, Jack."

She shut the door, and Jack stumbled back to the car. Forgiveness was happening.

Chapter 11

Pamela had no idea what was wrong with her. Jack had declined Thanksgiving dinner with her family, saying he had to help prepare a meal for the homeless at the shelter. She'd been surprised and quite frustrated. She hadn't wanted to invite him to begin with. She twisted her mouth. Okay, maybe a little bit of her wanted to invite him. But she couldn't believe he'd said no.

Sure, he'd asked to visit later that evening, around seven. And it was true, her family celebrated the meal a bit early at noon. And, yes, she knew the shelter was serving from two to four. Still, his absence irked her, and when Callie and Kirk offered to take the girls to see the new animated movie releasing that day, Pamela decided to pay a visit to her "husband" at his place of employment.

As she pulled into a parking space at the shelter,

her belly somersaulted. Maybe this hadn't been the best of ideas. She lifted her eyebrows when she spied a stringy-haired woman wearing layers of clothes beneath a dirty brown coat walking up the stairs of the shelter. Jack wasn't expecting her, and she wasn't used to being around homeless people. *God, how do people live like that? What happens that they end up on the street? There's government assistance everywhere. It doesn't make sense.*

She choked back a prayer. Since Jack arrived, she'd been doing that a lot more. Quick prayers. The fact that she'd succumbed to discussing things with God again really irked her, made her feel weak and needy. And yet she experienced moments of peace and security, as well. At the oddest times, she'd remember moments when God had provided for her and her children.

Like the time when the girls were small and she hadn't slept even half a night in a week. Her mom and dad had been down with the flu, Ben was still in high school and Kirk was at a cattle conference. Pamela had tried to care for her parents and the girls, but she'd hit a wall and was about to lose her mind when Greta had shown up with a meal and took the girls for the afternoon so that Pamela could take a nap.

Greta. The thought of her tore at Pamela's heart. Her friend had been taken from them in a car accident a few years ago. Her husband had remarried, to Greta's sister no less. It just seemed so wrong, and she couldn't understand why God would allow such a bad thing to happen to her friend.

Pushing away thoughts of provision and unfairness and how the two could possibly work together for God's will, Pamela opened the car door and walked toward the front of the shelter. She swallowed back her nerves as she made her way through the door.

"Welcome to The Refuge." Jack's eyes widened and his lips spread into a full smile. "Pamela."

"Hi, Jack, I..." What was she supposed to say? She drove over there because she was angry he didn't come to the family's Thanksgiving? That she wanted to see what was so important that he'd decline spending the holiday with the daughters he'd reunited with only a month ago?

"I'm glad you're here." He motioned her inside. "Come on in. I'd love to introduce you to some of my friends."

Pamela looked around. The shelter didn't look anything like she expected. The room was bright, and there were verses painted in big letters on the walls. Each round table had a bouquet of orange-and-yellow flowers in the center. The serving line reminded her of school, but the men and women standing behind it beamed with huge smiles as they handed each person a tray of food.

Jack took her hand, surprising her when he walked directly to one of the homeless men at a table closest to the canisters of iced tea and lemonade. "Steve, I'd like you to meet my wife."

The shaggy-bearded man grinned, exposing several rotted teeth. Though he seemed a bit confused, his eyes appeared kind enough. The grime that covered his face and hands and clothes made her want to take a step back. She hoped he wouldn't want to shake hands.

Instead, he clicked his tongue and winked at her. "Ain't you every bit as pretty as Jack here said."

He lifted his elbow and nudged Jack, and body odor

wafted to Pamela's nostrils. How could Jack stand this day in and day out?

"She is at that." Jack pointed toward the serving line. "I'm going to introduce her to Pastor Mark."

Steve didn't respond, but instead focused on his meal again. Jack guided her toward the volunteers then stopped when the front door opened again. He lifted his finger. "Be back in just a minute."

Jack walked to the door and greeted the woman. He asked her something, and she seemed hesitant, almost angry. He motioned to a pretty dark-haired woman who had been wiping off tables. The woman spoke with the homeless lady, who handed over the bag she carried on her shoulder. The volunteer went through the bag, then replaced all the contents and handed it to the homeless woman. She headed toward the serving line, and Pamela watched as Jack and the volunteer talked. Jealousy wiggled up her spine at the intensity in the dark-haired woman's gaze. No doubt the gal had her eye on Jack. *Well, he's my husband, lady. So back off.*

Heat warmed Pamela's face. Where had that thought come from? She didn't want Jack. Sure, it was great that he wanted to be part of the girls' lives, and the money he'd given them each week had been a huge help, but she'd already determined she didn't want the two of them to get back together.

She glanced at the volunteer. And yet she didn't want him to get with that woman, either. She lifted her shoulders when Jack and the lady made their way toward her. *Great.* She couldn't wait to the meet the gal.

Jack pointed to the woman. Of course, she was even more beautiful up close. "Pamela, this is Teresa. She's one of the volunteers."

The woman smiled, but Pamela could tell it was forced. Her body language mimicked Pamela's. Neither of them wanted to meet the other. Challenge warred within her gut as she extended her hand to the volunteer. "It's a pleasure to meet you."

"And you." Teresa narrowed her gaze just a bit. "I've enjoyed helping Jack get the shelter up and going."

"I'm sure *my husband* appreciated your help."

Teresa nodded and walked away, and Pamela looked back at Jack. His eyebrows were raised, and the left side of his mouth was lifted in a crooked grin. Her jealousy had been all too apparent. Pamela bit back a growl and looked away from him. "So, who else do you want me to meet?"

Jack walked into Pamela's parents' house. Mike greeted him with a handshake. "How'd the Thanksgiving meal go today?"

Tammie made her way into the room. "Pamela said you had quite a turnout."

"We did." Jack accepted her hug and nodded. "I was surprised Pamela came."

"God is always working."

Jack lifted his hands as he looked around the room. "Where is everyone?"

"Callie, Kirk and the girls should be back from the movie anytime," said Mike. "Not sure where Ben ran off to, and Pamela ran over to the cabin to get her apple crisps."

Jack licked his lips and rubbed his belly. It had been a long time since he'd enjoyed Pamela's dessert. "Apple crisps?"

Tammie nudged his arm. "She wouldn't admit it in a

hundred years, but if you ask me, she made them special 'cause she knew you were coming."

Jack's heart warmed. He hoped his mother-in-law was right. Worry settled in his gut when he thought of his last encounter with his younger brother-in-law. "Does Ben know I was coming over?"

Mike shook his head. "Never had a chance to tell him. Didn't tell us he was leaving…"

"Just turned around and he was gone," Tammie said. She frowned. "I'm worried about that boy. Something's not right."

Jack shared her fear. Once upon a time, he and Ben had been close. Jack would have grabbed Pamela's younger brother by the collar and asked him man-to-man what was going on. Yet another relationship he had ruined when he'd allowed the bottle to become his god. Jack patted Tammie's shoulder. "I've been praying for him."

The front door swung open and Emma and Emmy bounded inside. "The movie was awesome," squealed Emmy. She spied Jack and opened her arms. "Daddy!"

Emma waved. "Hi, Dad. Did you come to play games?"

"I sure did." He placed his hands on each of the girls' shoulders. "Why don't you tell me about the movie while we set up the game?"

Callie rested her hand on top of her growing belly. Fatigue traced her flushed face. "I'm whipped. I think I'll lie down for a bit."

Kirk kissed the top of her head. He covered her hand with his own. "Not even born yet, and the boys are already wearing out their mama."

Callie swatted his shoulder. "Kirk, stop doing that. We do not know if they are boys."

Kirk chortled. He wiggled his eyebrows, and Callie swatted his arm again. Jack remembered bantering with Pamela when they were dating and newly married. One day, he hoped to have the camaraderie again. The back door opened, and the scent of apples and cinnamon filled the air.

Emmy clapped her hands. "Apple crisps are ready."

Callie stopped, a grin gracing her face. "I think I have enough energy to eat a bit before I rest."

The family laughed as they walked into the kitchen. Jack looked at Pamela. Her face flushed when their gazes connected. Could it be because she'd made his favorite dessert or because she'd been jealous of Teresa earlier? If she'd let him, he could set her mind at ease about Teresa. The only women he was interested in stood in this kitchen.

Tammie took bowls out of the cabinets, while Pamela placed silverware and napkins on the counter. Kirk got out the vanilla ice cream, and Callie and Mike sat down at the table. Jack sat opposite them, and the girls plopped into seats on either side of him. Emmy grabbed his hand and nestled her cheek against his palm, and Emma grinned at him as she rubbed her hands together in anticipation of the dessert.

Pleasure trailed through him once everyone sat at the table together with apple crisps and ice cream in front of them. He'd longed for this, to be a true part of the family once more.

Closing his eyes, he took the first bite and savored the sweet, cinnamon-apple flavor. A memory filled his heart of Pamela making the dessert for him soon after they'd learned she was pregnant with Emma. He'd been confused and scared, and she'd tried to encourage him that everything would be all right. Her faith had been so strong and his so weak.

Opening his eyes, he looked at her. She studied him, and he wondered if she could read his thoughts. She nodded toward the dessert. "Good?"

"As always."

Emmy licked the back of her spoon. "I'm ready to play a game."

"Me, too." Emma placed the silverware in her empty bowl.

Taking the last bite, Jack stood and grabbed the girls' bowls, then set them in the sink. "I'm ready, too."

Kirk took Callie's hand. "I think I'll take my girl back to the house and let her rest a bit."

Callie didn't protest as she stood and leaned her head against his shoulder. "Tammie, I know I should stay and help with the dishes—"

"Nonsense. You cooked with Pamela and me all morning, then took the girls to the movie." Tammie kissed Callie's forehead and patted her stomach. "Go put my grandbabies to bed."

Emmy stuck out her bottom lip. "But we need another player. Who's gonna play if Callie and Kirk leave?"

Mike reached across the table and tapped Emmy's hand. "Your mama will play."

"No. I'm gonna help Mom clean up," said Pamela.

Mike pointed to his chest. "That'll be my job tonight. Go enjoy your family."

Jack held his breath as he waited for Pamela's response to her dad's words. A few weeks ago she would have glared at her father, proclaimed Jack not to be her family and left the room. But they'd made some progress since then. She'd softened toward him. Maybe she was even beginning to love him again. Or at least like him.

Pamela nodded. "Okay." She looked at the girls. "What are we going to play?"

The girls raced into the other room, and he and Pamela followed them. He wanted to take her hand, to feel the warmth of it once more in his own. But he didn't. The time would come, but for now he had to be patient.

Her phone buzzed, and she pulled it out of her front pocket. Jack spied the name Peter on the screen. That was the guy from the fall festival, the one who'd been her professor. No doubt the guy was interested in Pamela. Pamela snarled and shoved the phone back in her pocket without replying to the message. Jack sucked in a breath. He'd take that as a good sign.

The girls laid out the board game, and Jack sat beside Pamela at the card table her parents had set up in the living room.

"I'm yellow," said Emmy.

"Red," said Emma.

Pamela snatched the green and snickered. "Green."

He twisted his mouth and narrowed his gaze in jest at her. She knew green was his favorite color. He lifted his brows. "Then I'll have to beat you all with blue."

The girls cackled as Emma spun to see who would go first.

The front door opened, and Ben stepped inside. Jack couldn't get over how much the kid had grown. He wasn't a kid at all anymore. Several inches taller than Jack, with dark stubble covering his chin, Ben had grown into a man. A man with dark bags beneath his eyes and a hardened set to his jaw. He pointed to Jack. "What is he doing here?"

Pamela stood. "He's playing a game with me and the girls."

Ben squinted. "Really, Pamela? You're going to let him back into this house? Into your lives?"

Jack bit his tongue. Emma's face hardened, and Emmy's eyes filled with tears. He couldn't argue with Ben in front of them. *God, show me what to do.*

Mike and Tammie walked into the room. Mike glanced at the girls, then at Ben. "Son, I'm glad you're home. Why don't you come in the kitchen and get a bite of one of Pamela's apple crisps?"

Ben clinched his fists at his sides, and Jack feared he'd actually have to take a punch from his brother-in-law. Ben looked at the girls and, to his credit, his expression softened. "Sure, Dad."

He scowled at Jack as he walked past but didn't say another word. Jack tried to enjoy the game with Pamela and the girls, but the tension never lightened. Once the game ended, he hugged his daughters and told them goodbye, his heart heavy and his spirit saddened.

Chapter 12

After tucking the girls into bed for the night, Pamela marched the few yards back to her parents' house. Ben had no right to act that way in front of her children. She opened the back door and slammed it behind her. Spying her overgrown little brother sitting at the kitchen table eating another of the apple crisps she'd made, she pointed her finger at him. "How dare you?"

Ben swallowed the bite in his mouth, then lifted his hands. "How dare I what? Stand up for you and the girls?" He pointed toward the front door. "That man has no right to be anywhere near you all."

Heat washed over her. She was a grown woman, responsible for her life and her two children. "That is not for you to decide."

He pushed away from the table and stood, towering over her. "Don't you remember?" He tapped his fingertips against his temple. "Have you forgotten? The man never showed up to help Dad, Kirk and me on the farm when he said he would. Why? Because he was drunk or hungover."

"What's going on in here?" Their mother wrapped a robe around her and tightened the belt. Pins held her hair away from her cream-covered face.

Ben continued. "Or maybe you forgot that he left while you were pregnant, and you got so sick with worry and sadness that you went into labor early with Emmy. Not once, but several times. You'd cry and beg God to keep her safe while we chased after Emma and waited on you hand and foot."

Pamela crossed her arms in front of her chest. "I didn't know it bothered you so much to help me."

He smacked his hand against the table. "Of course I didn't mind. I'd do it again in a heartbeat. But would he?"

"Now, wait a minute, Ben...."

Their mother walked toward her brother. Her lips moved as she spoke to him, but the words jumbled together as Ben's question weeded its way through every fiber of her being.

The pain she'd suffered when Jack had left punched her in the gut. Yes, she'd told him to leave that night, but she never dreamed he would walk away for good. He hadn't fought to stay. For months, years even, she'd worried about him, feared for his very life. But she'd heard nothing. No phone calls. No cards or letters. No visits. Nothing until he'd started calling and hanging up two years ago.

"He wasn't here for any of it." Ben now addressed their mother. "Not when Emma potty trained or Emmy started walking. Not to teach them their alphabet or teach them to ride a bike. Not when they ran a fever or fought off a stomach bug. He. Was. Never. Here."

Pamela's heart squeezed. Ben's words were true. All of them. He'd abandoned her for all the girls' milestones to this point. He'd been attentive and reliable the past couple months, but could that really make up for the years he'd been gone? She'd never be able to really trust him. She didn't want to ever be so vulnerable again. When they'd said their vows, he'd promised to be beside her in the good and bad, in sickness and health. But he'd lied.

"You really think I'd give that man my heart again?"

The words spat from her lips, and her mother stopped talking to Ben and looked at her. Sadness wreathed her mom's features, and Pamela glanced back at her brother.

"You sure look to have stars in your eyes again," Ben said.

Pamela placed her hands on her hips. "He's paying me support, and he wants a relationship with the girls. I can't legally deny him that."

Mike walked in the back door and frowned. "What's goin' on in here?" He pointed to his wife, and Pamela watched a tear slip down her mom's cheek. "What's wrong with your mother?"

Ben growled. "I guess she had some cockamamie idea that Pamela should get back with Jack." He grinned. "But I suppose Pamela just set her straight."

Her father stared at her, and Pamela dipped her chin. Her brother's words and tone sounded disrespectful, and she didn't want to be lumped in on his side. Her dad glared at Ben. "I don't like the way you just spoke of your mother."

Ben rolled his eyes. "Dad, I would never say anything bad about Mom. It's just crazy to think that Pamela and Jack—"

Dad lifted his hand to cut him off, and Pamela bit her bottom lip. "You and I have something to discuss anyway. I'd planned to wait until tomorrow, but…"

He pulled an envelope out of the cabinet, and Ben's face blanched. Her brother stuttered, "Where did you get that?"

"It came to the house. I didn't look at who it was addressed to. I opened it and saw that my son has accumulated a great deal of debt."

Ben's jaw set in a hard line. "Think I'll head on back to school tonight."

"Now, son…" Tammie said, placing her hand on his forearm.

He pulled away and stalked out of the room and up the stairs. Her mom collapsed into tears, and her father gathered her into his arms. They seemed to have forgotten that Pamela was still standing in the kitchen with them.

"I'm so worried about him," her mom mumbled against her dad's chest.

Pamela lowered her chin again. She was worried about him, too. He hadn't been himself the past few visits. Always tired. Always grouchy. Always leaving the house.

"Let's pray for him right now."

Her dad took Pamela's hand in his; then her mother grabbed her other hand. Her heartbeat raced as her dad spoke words of thanksgiving and concern for their youngest child. She hadn't been able to share burdens with Jack. Not when the girls had been sick. Not when they'd had fusses with peers at school. She wanted it, this unity her parents shared.

Her father ended the prayer, then enveloped them both in a hug before Pamela said goodbye and headed back to the cabin. The house was quiet, with only the ticking of the clock sounding through the room.

She sat on the couch and wrapped her arms around her waist. She felt alone, more so than she had in a long time. She needed comfort. A warm embrace. Grabbing the soft afghan off the chair, she wrapped it around herself. The warmth didn't help. She had no one. Not Jack. Not God. She was utterly alone.

Jack placed the video game in the shopping cart filled with dolls, doll accessories and activity sets. Pamela pointed to the game. "Who's that for?"

"Todd. I think I'm just going to send money to Kari."

Pamela chewed her lip. "How is your family?"

"Dad hasn't spoken to me since he kicked me out of the house for good."

Pamela lifted her eyebrows, and he wondered when the time would come that he could share everything with her.

He continued. "But I talk to Mom about once a month, and I'm Facebook friends with Kari and Todd. We text and even Skype sometimes, so I keep up with them that way."

Pamela grinned. "I'm sure they've gotten big."

He nodded. "Kari's fourteen, looks like she's twenty." He blew out a breath. "Always has a boyfriend. And Todd's eleven, loves running cross country."

Pamela didn't respond, and he wished he could read her mind. His parents hadn't tried to contact his daughters since they'd moved to Texas. They didn't have much money anyway, but his dad also blamed Pamela for allowing his addiction to get out of hand. Something he never understood. Even when he was in the depths of the disease, he knew the fault for his problem rested on him alone.

She pointed to a pink-and-purple bike with a white basket on the front. "There's the bike I want to get the girls."

"One for each of them, right?"

"Yeah. I thought we could get little license plates with their names."

He liked the idea, as well, and Pamela pulled two cards from the clear plastic pouch. "We'll hand these to the cashier. She'll ring them up, and then we'll drive around back and someone will put them in the truck."

Jack motioned toward the filled shopping cart. "It's a good thing we brought your dad's truck."

Pamela flashed a smile that made his knees weaken. "I knew we'd need it."

After paying for the Christmas gifts and loading the bikes in the truck, Jack drove through a coffee shop and ordered peppermint mochas, then headed back to the farm. They unloaded the truck, then hid the presents in a storage space at the back of the cabin.

Jack gripped the bag containing his brother's video game. "I enjoyed shopping with you."

"I had a good time, too."

"When are the girls going to be home?"

"They're staying with friends."

Silence filled the room, and Jack knew he should simply tell her goodbye and leave. But he wanted her to ask him to stay.

"I made some cookies yesterday." She motioned toward his java. "We could eat a few with our coffees."

"Sounds terrific."

He followed her into the kitchen and sat at the small wooden table with only three chairs. A scrapbook, stickers, pens and colored paper sat in one corner. He glanced at the pictures of the girls on the page she'd been working on. They looked like birthday photos.

She placed a plate of cookies on the center of the table and handed him a saucer and a napkin. "I'm a little behind on the scrapbooking. Those pictures are from June."

He took a bite of the chocolate chip cookie. "Do you mind if I look at it?"

She shook her head. "Not at all."

He sucked in his breath when she pulled her chair beside him. She flipped to the front of the book and pointed out various photos. "This was Emmy's first day of kindergarten, and Emma heading to first grade."

They were almost the same height in the picture, but now Emma was much taller. The next picture was of Emmy's face up close. She pointed to an empty space where her tooth had been.

"First lost tooth?"

Pamela chuckled. "Yes. That child is quite a character."

"She is at that."

Pamela stood. "I'll go get the other scrapbooks, so you can see their baby and toddler pictures."

Jack praised God for Pamela's willingness to share about their lives. He'd feared Ben's outburst would place a new wedge between them, but she'd seemed more laid-back and willing to talk with him than she ever had before.

"Why don't you come in here? It's more comfortable on the couch," she called from the other room.

Jack would go anywhere she liked. He walked into the living room and sat beside her on the sofa. She opened the scrapbook, and he relished pictures of his girls as babies and toddlers. The pages were covered with proof of what a good job she and her family had done raising them.

He pointed to a picture of the girls on the back of a horse. Emmy's face shone with delight, while Emma looked down at the ground with her lips drawn in an exaggerated frown.

Pamela grinned. "That pretty much sums up their personalities, wouldn't you say?"

"From what I've seen, yes."

Pamela turned the page. Her fingers traced one of the photographs. "I missed you through all this."

Jack faced her. He took her chin in his hand and lifted her gaze to his. "I missed you so much, Pamela. Words will never express how sorry I am."

Her eyes filled with tears. With his free hand, he swiped the one that escaped. Her lips parted, and Jack couldn't stop himself. He lowered his mouth to hers. Softer and more delicious than he remembered, if that were possible.

She didn't pull away, and he traced her cheeks with his hand until his fingers found the softness of her hair. Everything in him ignited, and he moved closer to her on the couch. He longed for her touch. Yearned for her.

"Jack." Her voice sounded breathless, and he wanted to cover her lips again, but she pushed his chest. She touched her hand to her lips and shook her head. "Not ready."

He exhaled a deep breath, willing his heartbeat to slow down. "I'm sorry, Pammer."

She looked at him. Her expression was tender again, and he fought the need to take her in his arms once more. "It's okay."

"I want us to be a family again."

"I know."

"I love you, Pammer."

She stared at him. "I know you do. The best you know how, but I don't know if it's enough for me."

Jack frowned. What did she mean by that? He'd messed up, but he was proving he'd changed over and over to her. Emmy had welcomed him back. Even Emma had warmed to him.

She raked her fingers through her hair. "Jack, you better go."

Hurt, he didn't argue, but he leaned over and placed a firm kiss on the top of her head. "I will always love you."

His throat burned as he walked out the door and toward his car. The need for a drink washed over him. He pulled out his wallet, found the scripture he'd written on the card Jermaine had given him and prayed God would give him strength.

Chapter 13

Jack wrote his name on the guest sign-in sheet at the front desk of the girls' elementary school. He hadn't seen Pamela or his daughters for several days, and he missed them terribly. He hadn't succumbed to the urge to drink the evening he and Pamela had kissed, but he'd relived the moment each night when he closed his eyes. His need for her had jump-started with such fervor he couldn't stop thinking of her.

"Hello—" the secretary read his name from the sheet "—Mr. Isaacs." She handed him a visitor sticker. "May I ask the reason for your visit?"

"I'm here to have lunch with my daughters."

She nodded. "Wonderful. And who are your children?"

"Emma and Emmy Isaacs."

"Lovely girls." The lady sat down at her desk and

typed on the computer's keyboard. She turned toward him, frowning. "I'm sorry, Mr. Isaacs, but you aren't listed on the girls' contact lists. I won't be able to let you eat lunch with them."

Embarrassment warmed his neck and cheeks. He'd have never dreamed it would be so difficult to eat a meal with his children at their elementary school. Although when he thought of the senseless violent acts committed over recent years, he didn't mind going through the wringer to enter the building. "I've only recently moved back to town. I'm sure their mother just hasn't added me yet."

She shook her head. "I'm sorry. It's school policy. If Ms. Isaacs comes by the office or sends a note, then I'll be able—"

Jack spied one of his old classmates as she walked out of an office down the hall behind the receptionist's desk. "Brittany." He motioned her to the front.

The receptionist sat up straighter. "Mrs. Carter, I was just explaining to Mr. Isaacs—"

Jack laughed. "You and Walter got married. Good for you."

"Hello, Jack."

He took in her burgundy dress suit and white ruffled blouse. Her blond hair had been cut short. "So, what's Walter up to these days? Owen and I hang out as often as we can."

The receptionist spoke again. "I explained that I can't let him go to the lunchroom because he isn't on the contact list."

Realization smacked his face. "Are you the principal?"

"I am."

"That's great. I'm really happy for you." He leaned against the desk. "Is there anything I can do to be able to eat lunch with the girls? I told them I was coming. I didn't know about needing to be on a contact list."

Brittany nodded. "It's okay, Jack." She looked at the receptionist. "Call Ms. Isaacs. If she agrees to put him on the list, we'll let him in."

While the woman called Pamela, Brittany nodded to him. "It was good to see you, Jack."

She walked back to her office, and Jack wondered what she thought of him. She and Walter had been finishing their first year of college when he'd left. They probably deemed him lower than scum leaving Pamela and the girls. He couldn't blame them. When he thought on it too hard or let the past get to him, he'd call Owen or Jermaine for a reminder that he could only control what he did with his life now. And that he'd lain at the feet of Jesus.

The woman hung up the phone. She pushed a button that unlocked the door to the rest of the building. "You can go on back. The lunchroom is straight ahead on your left."

"Thanks."

He walked to the lunchroom and stood at the entrance. The place was filled with rectangular tables and children. It had seemed much bigger when he was a kid.

"Daddy!"

He heard Emmy's voice from the right side of the room. She stood up and waved for him to sit with her. As he walked toward her, he spied Emma sitting beside friends a few tables in front of Emmy's. He waved to her, and she offered a tentative wave back.

Emmy wrapped her arms around him in a hug. She

grabbed his hand. "You want me to take you through the lunch line?"

"How 'bout I just sit with you and visit? That way I can go see Emma at her table in a minute."

Emmy shrugged. "Okay." She patted the space beside her. "Sit, Daddy."

Jack sat beside her and looked at her friends. "You want to introduce me?"

Emmy pointed around the table. "Abby, Simon, Stephanie and Brody."

"It's a pleasure to meet all of you. What are you having for lunch?"

"Chicken noodle and grilled cheese," said Emmy.

"And carrots and broccoli," added Simon as he wrinkled his nose.

"Did you just move here?" asked Brody.

"I did," Jack responded.

"'Cause Emmy didn't have a daddy before," said Abby.

Emmy leaned forward. "Yes, I did. I just didn't know him yet."

Jack's neck and cheeks warmed again, and his hands began to sweat. Wiping them on his pants, he decided he wasn't going to get a break today. "I'm here now." He looked at each one of them. "I hear we're going to have a Christmas pageant in a few days."

The kids started talking all at once, and Jack tried to listen to who was going to be a present and a tree and Santa Claus and elves and Virginia and the editor of the newspaper. Shifting in his seat, he spied Emma's class line up to leave the lunchroom. He wondered if he should walk over to her and offer a high-five or give her a hug.

As shy as she tended to be, any show of affection might embarrass her too much.

She finally sneaked a peek at him, and he waved. She nodded just a tad, then faced forward in the line. He'd wait on the high-five or hug.

Emmy and her friends continued to talk about the pageant and who sang the loudest or had the most speaking parts, until their teacher called for them to line up. He gave Emmy a quick hug and kissed the top of her head. "I can't wait to see you in the pageant. You'll be the prettiest elf ever."

Emmy beamed. "Thanks, Daddy. I love you."

"I love you, too."

Jack opened the car door for Pamela. The ride to the school Christmas program had been a bit awkward, since they hadn't seen or spoken to each other since the night of their kiss. He had the added embarrassment of the school's receptionist calling to ask Pamela's permission to see their children at lunch. Still, he was glad she'd agreed to ride together. They planned to take the girls for ice cream after the program, and as uncomfortable as things might be at times, he wanted them all to be a family again.

They walked into the auditorium and Pamela pointed to a place in the middle near the front. "How 'bout we sit there?"

"Looks good to me."

Pamela stopped and talked with a couple he'd never seen before. She introduced them quickly, and he nodded a hello. After sitting down, she leaned toward him. The floral scent of her hair stirred his stomach, and he wished to lean closer and sniff his fill. "I don't see my parents. Do you?"

Jack scanned the audience. The place was packed so tight he wondered if it was a fire hazard. He shook his head. "I'm sure they're here somewhere. They left before we did."

His cell phone dinged, and Jack pulled it out of his front pocket. Kari had texted to tell him their mom had been feeling poorly again. Depression and muscle weakness seemed especially challenging during the most recent MS attack. He'd have to call her when he got home.

"Was that about the shelter?" asked Pamela.

He shook his head. "Mom's had an attack again. Seems they're coming more often."

Pamela touched the top of his hand. "I'm sorry, Jack."

"Thanks." He took her hand in his, and to his pleasure, she didn't pull away. "So, how do these programs work?"

Pamela chuckled. "As long as we don't have a repeat of two years ago, all will be fine." She smacked her knee. "I don't think I'll ever forget when Simon had an accident onstage, and Emmy saw it, panicked and then threw up all over him. He screamed and ran off the stage."

He lifted his eyebrows. "Sounds like quite a show."

She wiped her eyes. "I'll never get over it."

She giggled again, and Jack squeezed her hand. She'd curled her red locks, and they rested in waves below her shoulders. The deep blue turtleneck sweater enhanced the bright blue of her eyes. He leaned closer to her. "You look beautiful."

"Thanks." Her cheeks bloomed pink as she crossed her legs. He admired the knee-high heeled boots and khaki skirt she wore.

The lights dimmed, and Jack focused his attention to the front. Music started, and a bunch of kids rushed to the stage. One wore a pair of oversize glasses, a gray-haired wig and a long skirt, obviously playing the teacher or librarian or something. He searched for Emmy and Emma but didn't see them anywhere.

Pamela whispered, "Emma will be in the next scene. She'll be a reporter."

Jack nodded. "Does she have a speaking part?"

Pamela chortled. "Are you kidding?"

Jack grinned. "Guess not. What about Emmy?"

"She would, but second graders aren't allowed."

Jack nodded and watched as the scene changed, and Emma walked onto the stage with a group of kids. He pulled out his phone and took a picture. When Emmy ran out as one of Santa's elves a few scenes later, he took a picture of her, as well. The play ended, and the audience erupted in applause. He glanced at Pamela. "They did a great job."

"They always do. I don't know how Mrs. Lewis, their music teacher, accomplishes it, but she puts on a great play every year."

Once the children were dismissed, the girls bounded out from behind stage and hugged Pamela and Jack. He smiled at each of them. "You did a great job."

"Are we going for ice cream?" asked Emmy.

"Of course," Jack said. "Didn't I promise I'd take you if you did a great job?"

Emma twisted her foot. "Well, I did kinda trip when I went onstage the first time."

"I didn't notice it." Jack patted her shoulder. "I thought you did wonderful."

"Was I the best elf ever, like you said?" asked Emmy.

Jack tweaked her nose. "Of course you were."

"You know what that means." Pamela pumped her fist through the air. "Ice cream, here we come."

The girls cheered, and they all rushed to the car. Once at the ice-cream parlor, they sat at what had become their usual table with their usual orders.

"So, what did you think? I mean really," asked Emma.

"I think I'm looking at the best reporter and the best elf in the play," said Jack.

"I agree," Pamela offered.

The girls giggled as they dug into their desserts. Jack cherished each moment, committing each word, glance and smile to memory.

"We better head back. We've got school tomorrow," said Pamela.

"Aww," the girls whined in unison.

"Better listen to your mom." Jack stood, picked up their trash and threw it away. "Although I am surprised the program was on a school night."

"Second Thursday in December every year," said Pamela. "I think they schedule it like that because so many of the kids have multiple family gatherings to attend during the holidays."

Jack figured as much. Many of those gatherings were because the children had multiple families to visit. Mom's side. Dad's side. Stepmom's side. Stepdad's side. His stomach quivered at the idea of the girls visiting another man's relatives, and again he prayed God would reunite the family he had torn apart.

Once back at the cabin, Jack walked them to the front door. The girls gave him a quick kiss and then ran into the house and to their bedroom to change for bed. Jack pulled a check out of his front pocket and handed it to Pamela. "When can I see you all again?"

"You could come for dinner after church on Sunday."

Jack shoved his hands in his pockets. "I'll be there."

Pamela leaned against the door. "It was nice to watch the play with you."

"I'm glad I got to see it." He reached over and touched her hand. "I'm also glad I was with you."

She pushed away from the door. "Sorry, Jack. I have to do this one more time."

Before he could respond, she leaned forward, lifted her chin and pressed her lips to his. He sucked in a breath. He hadn't expected that, but he surely wouldn't deny her. Pulling her to him, he deepened the kiss, silently begging her to know the passion he felt.

She gasped and pushed away, then licked her bottom lip. The action stirred him, and he reached for her again.

"Night, Jack." Shaking her head, she rested her palm against his chest.

Fire seared through him. Jack bit back a growl as she stepped inside the cabin and shut the door behind her. He stalked back to the car and hopped inside. His phone dinged, and he pulled it out of his pocket. Another text from Kari.

He pressed her number on the speed dial. Kari sounded older than her years when she answered. "Hi, Jack."

"Hey, Kari. What's up?"

"Not Mom, that's for sure. She's pretty down this time. Depressed, I mean. Todd even had to help her get to the bathroom today when I was in the shower."

"Where's Dad?"

"Working all the time." Kari sighed. "Hiding if you ask me."

Jack's heart twisted. He wished he could visit his family, take some of the pressure off his siblings, if only for a few days. His dad had to work a lot of hours to pay for Mom's medical bills, but he did seem to work more than necessary when she was having an attack. Jack had come to realize his dad wasn't trying to avoid helping Mom, but avoiding watching her in pain.

"I wish I could come to Texas and see you all."

"Why don't you?" asked Kari. "Just fly out for a few days."

"If only it were that easy." He gave Pamela every spare penny he earned, and she deserved it. She was his wife, and the girls were his children. It was his responsibility and desire to provide for them.

"Mom's calling. I gotta go."

"Kari?"

"Yeah?"

"I'm praying for you all."

"We need it."

"I love you."

"Love you, too."

He pushed the end button and dropped the phone onto the passenger seat. As he drove back to his apartment, he lifted a prayer for his mom and dad, sister and brother, Pamela and their girls. With a heavy heart, he parked the car, then picked up the phone and dialed Jermaine's number. He needed some wise counsel. He might even call Owen afterward and see if his buddy was available to catch a movie or hit the bowling alley. Jack had a feeling he wouldn't be getting much sleep tonight.

Chapter 14

Once inside the building, Pamela pulled off her gloves and untied her scarf. The temperature had dropped. Snow flurries fell, dotting the ground. Though not a usual fan of the cold, she didn't mind the weather in December. The cooler air made her *feel* as if Christmas was coming in a little over a week. Made her want to listen to Bing Cosby singing "White Christmas" or watch Jimmy Stewart as he listened to his daughter share when angels get their wings.

Warmth flooded her as she remembered Christmas shopping with Jack. They'd had a terrific time buying for the girls. His eyes had lit with delight with each present she suggested, even the doll clothes. She had no doubt he regretted the time he'd missed with them. And he had changed. Just as he said.

Unbuttoning her coat, she recalled the kiss they'd

shared on the couch after the excursion. She'd yearned for the union she'd once known. She'd had the strength to deny the urges, but her mind replayed the kisses throughout the night and the next day. And the day after that.

Walking into Dr. Mays's classroom, her cheeks burned when she remembered kissing Jack again the night of the Christmas program. What had she been thinking? Leading him on was wrong, and she wasn't ready to get back together with him. Fear of giving herself to him again only to be left a second time made her sick to her stomach. Part of her wanted to trust, to just let go and give it a shot. The other part of her wanted to protect herself.

"Can you believe we're here?"

Pamela blinked away her thoughts and focused on the short-haired girl who'd just said something to her.

"None of my other classes met today. The tests were all online, and my papers were emailed."

Pamela smiled at her. They'd never spoken. She considered introducing herself, then decided there would be little point since it was the last class of the semester. "Dr. Mays is definitely old-school."

The girl huffed. "Try ancient-school. I haven't had to actually print a paper to turn in to the teacher since middle school."

Pamela laughed. "At least this should be quick. All he has to do is hand back our last assignment."

She growled. "I know. If I don't get a B on this paper, I'll have to take the class again." She shook her head. "I don't know if I can listen to him for another semester."

"I have to get a B in order to keep my scholarship."

Dr. Mays walked in and shut the door. Pamela sat up in the seat. The girl leaned over. "Good luck."

Pamela nodded. "You, too."

Dr. Mays opened his briefcase and pulled out their papers. He talked about enjoying the class and hoping they'd learned many financial management skills. Pamela tried to focus on his words, but her eyes and mind stayed focused on the stack sitting on the corner of his desk. If she got a B on this paper, she'd get a C in the class. Because she had As in her other classes, she could make the C and keep a 3.5 grade point average.

She rubbed her hands together. He needed to pass out the papers already. Surely he knew they were all about to explode from anxiety.

He picked up the stack. Pamela bit her bottom lip and offered a silent plea to God for a good grade.

"You're free to go when I give you your paper," said Dr. Mays. "Enjoy your winter break."

He paused. "Oh, yes, and for your convenience, I wrote your grade in the class on the top left corner." He chuckled, a sound that reminded her of a fake laugh. "No need to wait until final grades are posted on the web."

Pamela's heartbeat raced as he passed the papers to her peers. She closed her eyes when he laid the paper on her desk. Sucking in a breath, she opened them and smiled. She got an A. Glancing at the top left corner, her heart plummeted into her gut when she read D.

She furrowed her brows as she pulled the syllabus out of her folder. Checking each grade and calculating the average, the D didn't make sense. She should have a C in the class with no problem now that she'd gotten an A on the final paper.

The girl beside her pumped her fist in the air. "I did it." She held up her paper, showing a C on the assignment and a D in the class. "How 'bout you?"

Pamela shifted in her seat. "I'm going to have to talk with him. I got an A on the paper, but he's showing I have a D in the class. Doesn't make sense."

The girl stood. "Well, good luck again to you, and have a good break."

Pamela nodded. She'd kept each assignment and test for the class. Pulling them out of her folder, she recalculated the scores. *I should have a C.*

Her heartbeat raced, and her hands grew clammy as she waited for Dr. Mays to finish passing out papers. When the last person finally left, he walked back to his desk. She gathered her syllabus and papers and stood beside him. "Dr. Mays, I have a question about my grade."

He didn't look at her. "Grade's at the top."

"Yes, I know, but my calculations show I should have a C in the class, not a D."

He looked up, peering over the rim of his glasses at her. With an exaggerated sigh, he held out his hand. "Let me see."

She swallowed the knot in her throat and willed her heart not to beat out of her chest as he thumbed through her papers and punched the figures on his calculator. "Hmm," he said. "Your calculations do appear correct." He pulled a grade book out of his bag. "Let me see what I have written down."

She waited as he found her name, then tapped a place on the book. "This is why I love the old method of grading." He smiled at her. "I made an error, and since you kept all your papers, you were able to catch it." He wrote a number in the book. "I neglected to give you a score for an assignment." He tapped the second paper she'd written for him. "But you have proof of completion and a grade." He handed her the papers, then patted her back. "Great job. Congratulations."

Ignoring the fact that she felt as if she were a two-year-old being congratulated for using the bathroom correctly, she shoved the papers back in her folder and nodded to him. "Thank you, Dr. Mays."

He grinned. "Have a terrific break, Ms. Isaacs."

She nodded again as she turned and walked out the door. She could have mentioned that if he'd embrace the technological age that she still would have had proof of turning in the paper, probably more so, because it would have been time-stamped in the class's drop box. But she didn't. It was his class, and if he wanted to be old-school about it, that was his choice.

After wrapping her scarf around her neck, she pulled on her gloves. She smiled as the weight of the class finally lifted from her chest. She'd gotten a C. She would keep her scholarship.

Jack turned the key in the ignition of the shelter's van. He shook his head at Owen. "See. Nothing. No turnover at all."

Owen scratched his head. "Probably the starter, but I'm about as good with cars as a piano player with no fingers."

Jack scrunched his nose. "Where do you come up with these comparisons?"

Owen grinned and shrugged.

Jack hopped out of the driver's seat and walked back to the front of the van. He looked at the engine and all the various hoses and gadgets. "I don't want to call Pastor Mark. The electric bill was already a few hundred dollars higher because of the cold weather."

Owen shoved his hands in his coat pockets. "Yeah, but we're not doing much good by standing here in the cold looking at it."

"I know."

Out of the corner of his eye, Jack spied Steve sauntering up the sidewalk toward the shelter. Jack waved, and Steve picked up the pace.

"Whatcha got going on here?"

Jack pointed to the engine. "Looks like we need a new starter."

Steve pointed toward the seat. "Get on in there, turn her over and let me hear."

Owen lifted his eyebrows, but Jack did as Steve said.

Steve smacked his lips. "Yup. The starter. I can fix her up for ya if you get me the parts." He patted the side of the van. "She's an old girl. Don't need all that fancy machinery they put on these new cars, so I know how to fix her."

Jack chewed the inside of his mouth as Owen slowly shook his head left to right. Jack lifted his hands. "Steve, I don't have the parts you'd need."

Steve spat on the ground. "Ain't no problem. Take me on over to the auto parts store, and I'll get us what we need." He laughed, exposing his rotting teeth. "Course, you'll have to pay for it."

Owen pursed his lips, looking at Jack like he'd be crazy to consider it. And yet something in Jack's spirit wanted to give Steve a try. Homeless people were homeless for a reason, and they all had a past most people didn't know about. Exhaling a quick breath, Jack said, "Okay, Steve, let's go."

Steve took a step back. "Really? You gonna trust me to fix it?"

Jack narrowed his gaze. "You said you could."

Steve nodded. "I can. I can."

Jack pointed to his car. "Then let's go get the parts."

Owen looked at his watch. "I'd go with you, man, but I gotta get back to work."

"No problem," said Jack.

He whispered, "I'll say a prayer this works."

Jack grinned. "I'll be praying with you."

Jack opened the car door, and Steve got into the passenger seat. The stench overpowered Jack in the small space, and he wondered if his car would ever be the same.

Once at the auto parts store, Jack was all too aware of the stares of the customers as he and Steve picked up the parts he'd need. One woman took her young son by the hand and left the store altogether. Jack didn't blame her. People were often afraid of people who weren't like them, especially if they looked bad and smelled bad. But there was so much more to the homeless. He knew that firsthand.

After paying for the parts, Jack drove back to the shelter. He stood outside, his gloved hands shoved into his coat pockets. He couldn't believe Steve could stand to be tinkering on that van in the cold with no gloves at all. After a while, Steve stood to his full height and smacked dirty hands together. "That should do her." He motioned to the front. "Try her out."

Jack put the keys in the ignition and turned. To his surprise, the van roared to life. Steve chuckled as he smacked the hood shut. "Still got it."

Jack hopped out of the van and walked to Steve. "You were a mechanic, weren't you?"

Steve lifted his chin and pride lit his eyes. "One of the best in town."

"Why are you on the streets?"

Steve shrugged.

Jack studied his friend for a moment. "Come on. You deserve a treat."

Jack grabbed his arm and guided him into the shelter. He settled Steve into one of the chairs and went back to the kitchen and fixed two cups of hot chocolate. *God, show me the words to say. Lead Steve to You.*

He handed Steve a mug, then sat across from him. "Careful. It's hot."

Steve blew on the top. "Smells good. Ain't had hot chocolate in years."

Jack wrapped his hands around the mug, allowing the heat to warm his hands. "You know I was homeless for a while."

Steve squinted at him. "You were? How long?"

"About a year before I became a Christian and started working and living at the shelter."

"Hmph. Where at? Ain't never seen you around here." He pointed to his chest. "And I reckon I know everybody."

"Texas. A man named Jermaine led me to the Lord. I started working for him. Lived in a shelter called God's Hands."

"Hmph." He pointed to Jack. "Why was you on the streets? Seem like a smart fellow."

"I am a smart fellow. My guess is that you are, as well."

Steve lowered his gaze and took a long drink of the cocoa. It was still hot, and Jack knew the liquid had to burn going down.

Jack figured if he wanted to make any headway with his homeless friend, he'd have to lay his own life on the line. "I was stuck on the bottle," said Jack.

Steve clicked his tongue. "Yup. That'll do it." He pointed to his head. "Stopped taking my crazy meds. Used different drugs instead."

Jack nodded. He wasn't surprised. Sometimes Steve was lucid, like today. Other times his eyes were glazed and confusion dominated his expression. Mental instability, drugs or both.

"Why'd you stop taking your meds?"

Steve shuddered. "Side effects were awful."

"Maybe you just need to try different kinds or doses."

"Got tired of that. None of them worked, and when Janine died, I didn't care that they didn't work."

"Janine was your wife?"

Steve clammed up and took another drink of the hot chocolate.

Jack twirled his fingers around the cup. He had yet to take a drink, but his spirit was so heavy for Steve. He wanted to share, to convince him to accept the Lord, to change his life. He prayed for God to put the right words in his mouth. "You know what really turned my life around?"

Steve didn't respond.

Jack continued. "Jesus. When I accepted Christ as Lord of my life, everything changed. I was able to fight my addiction. My life—"

Steve slammed the cup on the table and stood to his feet. "Well, Jack, thanks for the cocoa. Glad to help you with the van."

Steve wasn't ready. Not yet. "Thanks again for fixing it."

Jack released a long breath as he watched Steve walk out the door. His friend wasn't ready, but that wouldn't stop Jack from praying.

Chapter 15

Pamela shook hands with Jermaine and Stella. Jack had talked about them many times over the past few months, but they looked nothing like she had imagined. She'd known they were African-American, but she'd envisioned a younger, more haggard-looking couple. They had to be in their late fifties, early sixties, but with their contemporary clothes and hairstyles, they reminded her more of her parents than workers in a homeless shelter. Jermaine's eyes twinkled with merriment, and she experienced an instant connection with him, but Stella seemed to hold her at arm's length. She studied her, and Pamela found herself wondering if the woman had doubts that she was good enough for Jack.

Jack glanced at her and Stella. "Jermaine wants me to go with him to the back. We'll be back in a couple minutes."

Pamela smiled, willing him to read her mind not to leave her alone with the woman. He didn't get the message, and Pamela clasped her hands together when she and Stella were left alone in the room.

Stella motioned to some chairs. "We could sit a spell."

Pamela nodded and sat across from Stella. She crossed her legs and folded her hands in her lap. She had no idea what to talk with the woman about, and she wanted to choke Jack for leaving them alone.

They'd had a wonderful dinner as a family on Sunday after church. Even Emma had looked forward to seeing Jack. When he'd asked her to meet the couple from Texas, she hadn't had the heart to say no.

"How are things between you and Jack?"

The woman's voice was stern, leaving no room to argue about responding to her question. "Good."

"You're not back together yet, though?"

Pamela shifted in the seat. That wasn't any of this woman's business. Stella might have a relationship with Jack, but she most certainly didn't have one with Pamela, and Pamela owed her no explanations. Still propriety required she answer the question. "No."

Stella leaned forward in the chair. "He tell you about his time with us?"

Pamela glanced at the door leading to the back of the building. What was taking them so long? Maybe she should just go check on them. She felt Stella's intense gaze and sucked in a breath as she responded. "No, he didn't."

"Have you asked?"

"No."

Pamela studied her fingernails. Sometimes she wanted to ask him what he'd done the eight years he was gone. Then she feared his answer. Feared he'd tell her the truth of it, and she'd be devastated. She inwardly chuckled at her thinking. She was such a fool. Claimed she didn't want him back but feared the truth would cement her desire to never allow him back.

"You wanna know?"

She stared into Stella's eyes. "I honestly don't know."

A slow grin spread over Stella's face, and, for the first time, Pamela spied kindness in her eyes. "Well, I'm gonna tell you a bit. That husband of yours lived with us at God's Hands for three years."

Surprise swelled in Pamela's gut, and she lifted her eyebrows. "What? That long?"

Stella pursed her lips. "Yep. That boy had spent a year before that pretty much on the streets. Living here, there and everywhere. Believe your husband said his parents had kicked him out for good."

Pamela crossed her arms in front of her chest, feeling uncomfortable that Stella kept referring to him as her husband. She hadn't realized he'd actually lived on the streets. The truth of it sent a shiver down her spine, and she stared at a bubble gum wrapper on the floor.

Stella continued. "He'd wandered into the shelter several times." She shook her head and clicked her tongue. "Knew that husband of yours was hungover most the time. Then one day this woman comes into the shelter. Has these two little girls."

She stopped talking, and Pamela looked up. Stella wiped a tear from her cheek with the back of her hand. "Well, I'll let him tell you the details. But that was the day he grabbed Jermaine and begged him to show him how to straighten up his life."

A huge smile spread over the woman's face and she

sat up straighter. "And my Jermaine led that boy to the only one who could cure him, Jesus Christ. After that, your husband cleaned up his act, attended meetings, started back to school, even lived at the shelter and worked for us."

Pamela's brow furrowed. "He kept living at the shelter?"

"Yep."

"But why?"

"Well, he was in school and trying to save every extra penny for you and the girls."

Emotion swelled within Pamela, threatening a display she'd prefer not to have in front of the woman. She jumped to her feet. "Excuse me, Stella. I need to use the restroom."

Pamela raced into the bathroom and turned on the faucet. After wetting a paper towel, she dotted her cheeks and forehead. Thoughts pelted her brain from every angle. He'd been sober for years before he'd called. Lived in a shelter to save money. He'd actually lived on the streets. Was kicked out of his parents' home. Who did he live with? What had he done? What had happened to him?

She closed her eyes. He told her he loved her every time they saw each other. Part of her wanted to love him again. In the depth of her heart, she knew she loved him. But knowing something and acting on it were different things. Maybe it wasn't safe to love him again. Her heartbeat sped up. Horrible things happened to homeless people, and drunk people made bad choices.

Pulling back her hair, she growled into the mirror. It would be easier to simply walk away, to tell him to get out of her life forever. But she knew he wouldn't. Even if she rejected him, he wouldn't leave the girls again.

The truth of that simmered in her heart. He wouldn't leave the girls. In her spirit, she knew he wouldn't. Blowing out a breath, she threw the paper towel in the trash can and walked out of the bathroom.

Stella placed her hand on Pamela's arm. "You all right?"

Pamela nodded.

"Talk to him."

"I'm gonna have to."

Jack gazed at Pamela across the booth. She looked beautiful in the silky green blouse and dark skirt. A thin strand of pearls hugged her long, creamy neck. She'd pulled her red mane up into some kind of knot, but long strands fell against her ears and neck. Though she rarely wore dark makeup, she'd put some dark green shadow on her eyelids that made her blue eyes almost glow in the dim light.

He still couldn't believe she'd agreed to go on a date with him. Before they'd left, Stella had encouraged him to ask Pamela to spend some time just the two of them. He'd thought the older woman crazy, but maybe he'd been dragging his feet, trying too hard to prove he'd be a good father. Maybe he needed to focus more on the romance he hoped they'd share again.

The waitress arrived at the table, and they ordered steaks, baked potatoes and salads. When the woman walked away, Pamela placed her napkin in her lap. "This is very nice, Jack."

"I'm glad you agreed to come. I want us to spend time together as a couple."

"I know."

She averted her gaze, and Jack took a drink of his sweet iced tea. He pondered what he should say to her. Nothing too heavy. They just needed to enjoy spending time together. He cleared his throat. "Have all your grades been posted?"

"Mmm-hmm. Four As and one C. Exactly what I expected."

"That's terrific. Three semesters to go, right?"

"That's right."

She reached for her glass and took a drink. Jack clasped his hands on the table. The waitress returned and filled their glasses. Pamela still didn't look at him as she took another drink.

He tried again. "Jermaine and Stella bought me a bus ticket to Texas, so I can visit my family." He wanted to add that he'd love for her and the girls to join him, but he knew better than to ask. Yet.

"That's nice." She traced the rim of the glass with her fingertip. "Is it round-trip?"

He stared at her until she finally looked him in the eye. "I'm never leaving again."

She nodded, and the waitress arrived with their food. He took Pamela's hands in his and allowed his thumbs to caress her palms as he prayed over their food. With the amen, Pamela pulled back her hands and started eating. He tasted little as he shoved bites into his mouth. What was wrong with her? He never knew from one moment to the next how she would behave. He'd never been a big fan of roller coasters, and this was one he especially wanted off.

She looked at him and swallowed. She wanted to ask something. Her anxiety was obvious. He wished she'd just spit it out. "Pamela, if there's something you'd like to—"

"Stella talked to me about your past."

Jack blinked and looked at her. "What about it?"

"About your living at the shelter. That you were actually homeless."

"That's true." Jack wiped his mouth with the napkin. "I'll tell you anything you want to know. I've been waiting for you to ask."

Pamela peered at him. "Where did you go when you left?"

"I moved in with my parents, and when I wouldn't stop drinking, they kicked me out. I lived with a buddy before he kicked me out, then back with my parents, then I ended up shacking up in a raggedy tent on the outskirts of town."

Pamela chewed on her bottom lip. He could imagine everything she'd want to know, but he'd wait and let her ask.

"How did you end up at Jermaine and Stella's shelter?"

He remembered the first time. The temperature had dipped below freezing the night before. He'd almost died in that tent. When he hadn't, he'd wandered into town and seen God's Hands. "Got cold. I knew I'd freeze if I didn't find better shelter."

She nodded. "Stella mentioned a woman and two girls?"

Pain laced through Jack's veins. When he closed his eyes, he could still see their faces. Forever he'd wonder what had happened to them. He nodded. "The woman." He motioned to Pamela's hair. "Her hair was a little lighter than yours. She had two little girls with her." He shrugged. "So close in age they might have been twins."

Pamela interrupted him. "They reminded you of me and the girls?"

He nodded. "The woman had two black eyes. The girls were too thin. Fear filled their eyes. Their dad had…" He shook his head. "I'll never forget the look in their eyes." He took Pamela's hand in his. "It was that night I realized I was the lowest of sinners, and I needed God. I wanted to change, and I wanted to be a good husband to you and a good dad to the girls. I realized only God could change me."

Pamela looked down at the table. "Did anyone ever hurt you? You know, while you were homeless?"

"No."

"Did you ever hurt anyone?"

"You mean besides you and the girls and my family? No. I never physically hurt anyone."

Her voice sounded little louder than a whisper. "Did you…were there other women?"

"No."

She lifted her chin and looked into his eyes, daring him to lie to her. He wished she could read his mind.

He shook his head. "No."

She nodded and excused herself to the restroom. While she was gone, Jack paid for their meal and prayed that God would reunite them as husband and wife. When she returned, she didn't say anything, and since he was unsure what he should say, he helped her into her coat, then put on his own and guided her to the car.

The car ride home was quiet, and Jack begged God to give him words to say, but his spirit remained quiet, so Jack waited. When he pulled in front of the cabin,

Pamela turned in her seat to face him. Tears pooled in her eyes, and he lifted his hand to wipe them away. She stopped him.

"I loved you, Jack. With everything in me."

He remembered how she'd fawned on him, almost worshipped him while they dated, and the many times he'd taken advantage of her affections. "I don't deserve another chance, Pamela. I know that, but I do love you, and I'm asking for the chance to make it up to you. To start again."

Her neck moved as she swallowed. "A lot happened while you were gone."

He nodded and waited for her to finish.

She lifted her chin. "I learned to be independent, to take care of myself and the girls."

He grabbed her hand. "And you've done a great job. I'm so proud of you. The girls are—"

She pulled her hand away and lifted it to stop him. "You've changed, Jack. There's no doubt about that, and I believe you will be a great dad for the girls now."

Dread filled his heart as she wiped the tears from both eyes. She grabbed the door handle. "But you and I can't happen. I just…I just can't ever feel that way again. I won't allow it."

She didn't give him time to respond as she yanked open the car door, then raced inside the house. He closed his eyes and dipped his chin as sadness washed over him.

Chapter 16

Jack pushed End on the phone and covered his face with his hands. His mom had passed away. Unexpected massive heart attack. He dropped onto the chair, tears streamed down his cheeks, as Kari's sobs echoed through his mind. Todd and Dad hadn't spoken to him. His sister said they were too stunned and devastated.

Falling to his knees, he planted his face into the seat cushion. *God.* He didn't know what to pray. Didn't have the words. Didn't know his feelings. His heart.

He wanted a drink. Desperately. He licked parched lips. He couldn't remember the last time the desire had been so strong. New tears flowed as he thought of what a miserable son he'd been. How he'd disappointed her time and again.

Gripping the sides of his jeans, he tried to fight the urge to yank the keys out of his pocket and drive to the nearest liquor store. *God.* The desire was strong. So strong.

He'd failed his mom. The last time he'd seen her he'd been drunk. Sure, he'd talked with her many times since sobering up, but actually seeing her face, giving her a hug and kiss. He thought of his brother and sister. If it weren't for social media, he wouldn't even know what they looked like. Probably wouldn't have communicated with them at all.

He was the lowest of the low. The chief of all sinners. He balled his hands into fists. Pamela had rejected him. She'd made it clear she'd never take him back. He needed a drink. Licking his lips, he could almost taste it. *God, help.*

The office door opened. Hands touched his shoulders. He looked up into his old drinking buddy's face. Owen frowned, concerned. "Jack, what's wrong?"

"My mom. She died."

"Oh, no."

Owen helped him to his feet and wrapped one arm around his shoulder. He prayed out loud for peace and strength for Jack and his family. Jack's heartbeat slowed and his mind cleared more with each word from his friend's mouth. When Owen finished the prayer, he squeezed Jack's shoulder. "What can I do to help?"

"You just kept me from hitting the liquor store."

"Not me. God kept you."

Jack knew it was true. God had proven to be stronger than his weakness. He'd provided what Jack needed when he needed it. He only had to rest and trust in his Savior. "If you'll call the bus station and find out the soonest I can get a ticket, I'll make some calls to let everyone know I have to leave."

Owen nodded. "Consider it done."

Jack called Pastor Mark, who assured him the shelter would be cared for, and then he left a message with Jermaine that he'd have to use the ticket voucher sooner than expected.

Exhaling a quick breath, he called Pamela's cell phone. He hadn't talked to her since their date. Her voice mail picked up and he wondered if she'd avoided his call or if she was truly busy. A beep sounded. "Pamela, I'm going to have to leave for a few days. Mom died unexpectedly of a heart attack." The words caught in his throat, and he coughed. "Call me if you need anything. Give the girls a hug and kiss for me. Tell them I love them."

He wanted to tell her he loved her, as well. That no matter how she felt, he believed in the vow they'd made. He'd defiled and made light of it for years, but he was a new creation in Christ, and because of that he couldn't give up on his love for Pamela. He didn't even want to.

Ending the call without saying the words, he turned to Owen. "What time do I leave?"

"You've got an hour."

"Better pack fast. You mind to take me to the station?"

"You know I don't mind."

Once he was ready to go, Owen drove him to the station. On the bus ride, Jack alternated between napping and reading the Bible and commentaries on God's word. He'd have to keep his mind filled with scripture to make it through the next several days. Every hour he checked his phone. Pamela hadn't responded to his message. Closing his eyes again, he tried not to think about it. Tried not to think about his hurting family or never being able to talk with his mom again while on earth.

After finally arriving in Texas, he stepped off the bus and saw his dad, Todd and Kari waiting on the platform. Emotion overwhelmed him as they wrapped their arms around him.

"You're home," his dad muttered.

"I'm sorry I didn't see her," Jack mumbled, trying to hold on to a semblance of composure.

"She was proud of you, Jack," said Kari. She looked so grown-up with her light hair cut short and makeup on her face. He knew she'd carried the brunt of caring for their mother. She'd had to grow up fast.

He pulled Todd into an embrace. He'd been a mama's boy, and Jack knew her death hurt to the core of his being.

His dad scratched the day's growth of hair on his face. "She was proud of you, Jack. We both were."

Kari poked his arm. "I wanna see those nieces of mine. You haven't put any pictures of them on Facebook."

Jack shrugged. "Well, it's not quite—"

"I know. It's not quite that easy yet. But surely you have some on your phone."

"I do." Jack reached into his jacket pocket. His phone wasn't there. He checked his other pocket and his jeans. No phone. "I must have dropped it."

He jumped back on the bus and searched the seat he'd been in. Still no phone.

"Can I help you, buddy?" asked the bus driver.

"Yeah. I think I left my phone on the bus."

The man held up a cracked black iPhone. "This it?"

Jack's heart sank. "Yeah." It was the one the church provided for him.

The bus driver shook his head. "A fellow stepped on it in the aisle. Must have fallen out of your pocket when you stood up. Hope you had insurance."

He didn't, and he definitely didn't have the funds to replace it. He had a small emergency fund, but he wouldn't be able to get to it until he went back to Tennessee. He took the phone. "Thanks."

Showing the phone to his dad and siblings, he cocked his head. "Guess I can't show you any pictures."

"That stinks," said Kari. "Maybe we'll have a chance to run to—"

Jack stopped her. "It's okay. I want to spend time with you, not worry about phone calls. I've notified everyone where I am."

He wished he could have talked with Pamela in person. He could try her again from his parents' phone. He frowned. Except he didn't know her number. It was programmed into the phone. *I'll only be gone two days. She has a message on her phone. I'll spend this time focused on Dad, Kari and Todd.*

Pamela tied the bow on the present, then set it to the side. She picked up one of the books she and Jack had bought for Emma and set it on the wrapping paper.

Her heart was heavy. She knew Jack had left a message on her phone hours ago, but she hadn't had the courage to listen to it. All night she'd tossed and turned, replaying their last conversation. He'd been honest with her. She knew him. She could tell.

Folding the paper over the book, she then pulled off a piece of tape and stuck it on the wrapping. But then, honesty had never been a problem for Jack. He'd told the truth many times, almost to a fault. Like the time he'd admitted a dress she'd just purchased and loved made her look like a chocolate cupcake. *Which is why I know he truly loves me.*

"You're awful quiet tonight," said Callie.

Pamela glanced at her sister-in-law. Even in her nursing scrubs, Callie radiated happiness. "Just got a lot on my mind."

"Jack?" her mom asked.

Pamela really didn't want to talk about it with them. Her mom kept trying to talk her into "giving love another chance." Which was easy for Mom to say. Dad had never drank and left her with two kids. He'd been her hero from the moment the two of them said their I dos.

And Callie was eaten up with happiness. Something she deserved. Besides, Pamela didn't want to burden her pregnant sister-in-law.

Pamela shrugged, knowing she had to answer her mother. "Of course it's Jack."

"Mom!" Emma pounded on the bedroom door. "What are you all doing in there?"

"We're wrapping Grandpa's presents." She pointed to a couple of boxes behind her and whispered, "That's the truth."

Emma's giggles sounded through the door. "Don't wrap Dad's. Emmy and I want to do it."

"Okay," Pamela called.

Callie grinned. "So, what did y'all buy Jack for Christmas?"

"Emmy got him a tool set, and Emma got him a flannel shirt." Pamela snorted and rolled her eyes. "Like he doesn't have enough of those."

Her mom and Callie chuckled. Then Tammie asked, "Did you get him something?"

She shook her head.

Callie patted Pamela's leg. "She doesn't have to get him anything. The man's only been back in Bloom Hollow a few months. Pamela can take her time deciding how she feels about him."

Pamela smiled and mouthed "thank you" to her sister-in-law. Wrapping a ribbon around the present, discontent pricked at her. She knew how she felt. Her heart knew. Her mind knew. Even her spirit nudged her to just trust God with Jack again. But she'd held on to her fear of vulnerability for so long. First Jack left; then Greta died. She'd covered the fear with bitterness and independence, and it had served her well for the past few years.

She thought of Emma's struggles with anger and bitterness, how she used to snap at her sister and how Emma seemed to hide within herself when she felt uncomfortable. She'd wondered if Emma's change in personality had been a direct result of Pamela's hardened spirit the past few years. Since Jack had returned, Emma's disposition had changed. Her inner turmoil seemed to have lessened, and she acted more like a little girl again. *Maybe the fear I've clung to hasn't served me so well after all.*

"Mom!" Emmy pounded on the door. "I messed up your phone."

"What?" Pamela touched her jeans pocket. She'd forgotten she'd told Emmy she could play a game on it.

"I don't know what happened," wailed Emmy. "All of the sudden Daddy's voice was on the phone, but he wouldn't answer me. So I pushed the talk button, but he didn't talk, so I pushed the end button, and he still didn't talk."

With Emmy crying on the other side of the door, Pamela looked up at the clock. "It's almost bedtime. I think I'll take the girls back to the cabin, get their baths and put them to bed."

"No problem," said Mom. "Give them a kiss for me."

"And me," said Callie.

Pamela walked out of the bedroom and took the phone from Emmy. She bit back a growl when she realized her younger daughter had deleted Jack's message. Shrugging it off, she knew he'd call again within the hour to tell the girls good-night.

They walked to the cabin, the girls took baths and then each read a book to Pamela. She looked at her cell phone. Jack still hadn't called, and it was past their bedtime.

Concern wrinkled Emma's brow. "Did Dad forget to call?"

Pamela winked. "I'm sure he's working on something at the shelter and forgot." She handed the phone to Emma. "Why don't you call him?"

Emma pushed the contact, waited a moment then handed the phone back to Pamela. "It's his voice mail."

Pamela kissed each of the girls. "I'm sure he's just busy. We'll talk to him tomorrow."

After walking out of the room, Pamela placed her hand against her chest. Something was wrong. She could feel it. She called Jack's number again, and her heartbeat sped up when his voice mail picked up immediately. She called Owen's number. No answer. She tried again. Still no answer, but this time she left a message. She tried Pastor Mark. Straight to voice mail, just like

Jack's phone. After leaving a message, she called the shelter. No answer.

She gripped a chunk of her hair with her hand as she walked to her bedroom and shut the door. Was no one available to answer the phone? She played with her phone, trying to find the message Emmy had deleted. She dropped the phone on the bed. It was no use. Flopping on her belly, she covered her head with a pillow as thoughts shot through her mind. He'd been so hurt when she'd stepped out of the car. What if he'd been in an accident? What if he was drinking? What if he left again?

Fear rose in her throat and pounded her head. She loved him. She punched the bed with her fist. *God, I don't want to love him. I don't want to feel vulnerable again.*

Who are you really afraid of?

Her spirit wailed within her. She knew the source of her fear. God. He allowed bad things to happen. Like husbands to walk away and friends to die in car accidents. He allowed those things.

But why, God? Why do bad things happen? I served You, and I was a good wife to Jack. And Greta, too, Lord. She loved You with all her heart.

Scriptures flooded Pamela's mind. *My ways are not your ways. God gives and takes away. With the faith of a mustard seed, you can move this mountain.*

She sat up in the bed and hugged her arms around her waist. Faith. She wanted faith. Her heart clenched, and her breath stuck in her throat. Once upon a time, she'd trusted him with her whole heart.

Scriptures flowed through her mind again. *Faith of a child. Were you there when the earth was formed? I have a plan for you. All things work together for good. Trust Me.*

Pamela blew out a breath and looked up at the ceiling. "I give up, God. I can't do it. I can't fight You anymore. I don't understand everything." She shook her head. "I don't, but I'm going to trust You anyway."

After lying back in the bed, she closed her eyes. A peace she hadn't known for far too long enveloped her like a heavy, warm blanket. Soon she was fast asleep.

Chapter 17

Jack held his sister and brother tight as the men lowered their mother's coffin into the ground. Their father stood a few feet away from them, holding a bouquet of their mother's favorite flowers in one hand and her wedding ring in the other.

A few of Dad's coworkers had attended the funeral, as well as Kari's boyfriend and a couple of Kari and Todd's friends from school. Now the family stood alone, the rain pouring down as if a bucket dropped water from the heavens. The weather fit their demeanor and somehow made the tears easier for Jack.

He hated that his suitcase was packed and loaded in the trunk of his dad's car. They'd had a good two days catching up and sharing memories. He and his dad had made amends, and he hoped one day he could bring Pamela and the girls to Texas for a visit. At least the girls.

With the coffin in place, Todd took their dad's hand, and they walked in silence to the car. He'd miss his mother, but he would see her again one day in heaven. His heart ached for his dad and siblings. Mom had taken them to church when she was able, but Dad never shared her sentiments about faith. Jack knew Todd and Kari knew precious little about the Lord. *God, help me be a light to them.*

They didn't talk as his dad drove to the bus station. He didn't want to leave so soon. They couldn't even share the spaghetti and meatballs Dad's coworkers had brought to the house. But he couldn't afford to stay another day. And he missed Pamela and the girls. He needed to wrap his arms around them and tell them how much he loved them.

Once at the station, he hugged his sister. "You look so much like Mom." She cried into his chest. "Absolutely beautiful. I hope you'll go to church with your friend. Mom would want you to know Jesus." She didn't argue, simply nodded against his shirt.

He grabbed his little brother with his other hand. Unlike his sister, who looked years older, Todd looked closer to Emma's age than his own. "Hang in there. Call me anytime you want."

Todd wiped his eyes with the back of his coat sleeve. "I will."

His dad grabbed his hand and patted his shoulder. "I really am proud of you, Jack. You straightened up."

"God straightened me up, Dad." He glanced at his sister and brother. "Take them to church. You know Mom would want that."

His dad's eyelids brimmed with tears as he nodded. "I will."

With one last hug for each of them, Jack got on the bus. The ride from Texas back to Tennessee seemed especially long, and Jack wished he had his phone so he could call the girls. He tried to sleep, then attempted to read, but his mind whirred with one thought after another.

He might never be able to have Pamela as his wife again, but he would be a father to the girls. They'd have to discuss when he could pick them up and how often. Worry over the conversation weighed heavily, but he could never walk away from them again. Life was too short, too precious.

With the bus arriving back in Tennessee well past midnight, he didn't try to find a phone to reach Owen. Instead, he'd decided he would take a cab back to his apartment. The next morning he'd check on the shelter, then head to the nearest store to purchase a new phone.

The cab pulled up at the apartment and he changed his mind. Giving the driver the address of the shelter, he decided he'd shower and sleep there. He was anxious to make sure everything had gone all right since he'd been gone. He'd missed hamburger night, Steve's favorite night of the week, and he wanted to be sure his friend knew Jack hadn't left for good.

Once at the shelter, he walked into his office and dropped his bag on the floor. The couch looked more inviting than it ever had before. His shower would have to wait. He had to shut his eyes for a few hours or he wouldn't be able to make it through the next day.

Taking a blanket and pillow out of the closet, he made a makeshift bed. He pulled off his shoes and untucked his shirt. He offered a quick prayer for rest, for peace for his dad and siblings, and for the opportunity to see his girls tomorrow.

He smiled as he realized how much he felt at home back in Tennessee. God had pulled him out of the mire and brought him back to the place He had planned for him. *I can trust You with Pamela, Lord. Whether she ever loves me again or not, I entrust her to You.*

To no avail, Pamela slathered makeup on her red, swollen eyelids. Giving up, she tossed the eye shadow brush into the cosmetic bag. She pulled her hair through a ponytail holder. Staring at her reflection, she grunted. This was not how she wanted to look when she saw Jack again for the first time.

But she couldn't help it. She'd cried for two days straight. She'd yielded her life and fears back over to Christ, and each time she heard a Christian song or opened her Bible or voiced a quick prayer, she burst into tears again.

And Jack. She blew out a breath. Owen had finally called her back and told her that his mother had passed away and he'd taken a bus to Texas for the funeral. Her heart broke for him. Not only had Pamela finally admitted to herself and to God that she loved her husband, but she'd had to live for two days knowing Jack had mourned his mother's passing believing she wanted nothing to do with him.

Tears filled her eyes again, and she grabbed a tissue, blotted them then pointed at her reflection in the mirror above the bathroom sink. "You've got no cry left in you, woman. Get a grip."

Sucking in a deep breath, she tugged at the bottom of her long flannel dress, then adjusted the brown belt around her waist. She pulled her cowboy boots over chestnut-colored leggings and walked out of the bathroom.

"Mom, are you all right?"

Pamela's lower lip quivered at Emma's soft words and concerned expression. She wrapped her arm around her child's neck and kissed the top of her head. "I am perfectly fine. You and Emmy are going to Grandma and Grandpa's while I run some errands."

She nodded, but Pamela knew the child still feared something wasn't right. Grabbing the oversize umbrella, she walked the girls to the main house before dashing to her car. She kept the radio off on the drive to the shelter, fearing if she listened to Christian music she'd start blubbering again.

Her mind stayed in constant prayer mode. She didn't even know what she was thinking or wanting or planning to do or say. She simply begged God to show her when she got there.

She pulled into the parking lot beside the shelter. It was early and rain poured down in what seemed like solid sheets, but she knew the workers would be serving breakfast. She gazed into the rearview mirror and patted the corners of her eyes. Owen said Jack's bus was supposed to have arrived late last night. She knew he'd be at The Refuge first thing in the morning.

She gripped the strap of her purse. She still didn't understand why he'd turned off his phone, why he hadn't called the girls for two days. The what-ifs that flitted through her mind had ransacked her heart, making her physically ill each time she allowed herself to think about it.

Pushing the car door, she opened the umbrella and

made her way toward the building. *He'll probably be at the door, greeting people.* She sucked in her breath as she walked up the steps and opened the door.

Her heart sank. Teresa smiled at her and shook her hand. Even wearing a plain red sweatshirt and jeans, the woman's dark hair and eyes made her look naturally gorgeous. "Hi, Pamela. What brings you here today?"

"I came to see Jack. Is he back from Texas?"

"He is. I believe he's in the office. Asleep the last time I checked."

Jealousy trickled down Pamela's spine at the idea of Teresa being in his office with him and knowing he was asleep there. And what if Jack wanted her to be in there with him since Pamela had rejected him so completely?

She blinked several times. *I'm going crazy. Absolutely losing my mind. God, help me get a grip.*

Pointing toward the office, Pamela said, "I'll just go back there and check on him."

After taking a few steps, a tall, lumbering man stepped in front of her. Pamela placed her hand on her chest as she looked up. The man smiled, exposing rotting teeth. His eyes twinkled with kindness, and she remembered she'd met him before. "Steve, right?"

He tugged at his shaggy beard. "That's right, miss. And you're Jack's wife, ain't ya?"

"I am."

He clicked his tongue. "I sure did miss him the last couple days. He didn't leave us for good, now did he?"

She shook her head. "I don't believe so." She opened her mouth to tell him that Jack was apparently in the office; then she stopped herself. Maybe Steve wasn't supposed to know Jack was in his office.

"Well, when you see him, tell him ol' Steve asked about him."

"I will."

With a quick wave, she walked past him, down the hall and toward the office. She knocked gently, but no one answered. She turned the doorknob. It wasn't locked. Taking a quick breath, she opened the door.

Jack started and jumped off the couch. His jeans and shirt were rumpled, and his hair stuck out in various spots. Bloodshot eyes seemed to try to focus on her as he wiped his face with his hand. "Pamela!"

Her heartbeat skipped, and thanksgiving flooded her. He was back in Tennessee. Safe. Nothing terrible had happened to him. She could love him and be there for him through the grief of the loss of his mother. She could...

Out of the corner of her eye, she spied a bottle on the desk. A tremor shot through her body when she turned and saw the half-empty liquor container. She looked back at him. Bloodshot eyes. Messed-up hair. Sleeping in his clothes.

He'd been drinking.

She smacked her hands against her thighs. "How could you? How could you come back into our lives after all these years, profess love to all of us then start drinking again?" She leaned forward and pointed at him. "Maybe you never gave it up." She smacked her thigh again and threw back her head. "Maybe you've been drinking all along, and I'm just a complete idiot."

Balling her fists at her sides, she stared at the framed picture of a wooded area with a stream that hung behind the filing cabinet. "And I came here to tell you I wanted to try…that I'd given my fears to God…and that you and I…"

She peered at him. Confusion ruled his expression. The hangover was clearly keeping him from understanding a word she was saying. "I can't believe I was such a fool."

He reached toward her, but she opened the door and walked out of the office. Some woman stepped beside her and asked where she could use the restroom. Pamela ignored her and walked to the door.

"Is everything all right?" asked Teresa.

"No." Pamela stalked out of the building without another word, fearing she'd tell the woman to take Jack to Timbuktu for all she cared.

Cold rain smacked against her head and face. She didn't care. Maybe it would simmer down her fury a degree or two.

She lifted her face to the heavens and closed her eyes against the rain. "God, I want to trust You. Help me."

Chapter 18

Jack raked his fingers through his hair. Where was he? What just happened? He looked around the room. His office. Looked down at his clothes. He'd gotten home from Texas late last night. He hadn't slept well for days, and exhaustion must have sent him into a deep sleep.

He glanced at his desk and frowned. Why was a liquor bottle there? He peered down at the bottle. A note sat beneath it. One of the volunteers had found it hidden beside the bed where one of their regulars slept. They'd warned John multiple times when he'd come in hungover that he couldn't bring alcohol into The Refuge. *He must have sneaked it in while I was gone. And Pamela thought it was mine.*

He had to stop her. He yanked on his shoes, then scooped up the note and shoved it in his pocket. Feeling a stick of gum in the pocket, he pulled it out and shoved the piece in his mouth. He desperately needed a shower, a change of clothes, to brush his teeth, but all that would have to wait.

Grabbing his coat off the chair, he threw it on as he raced out of the office. He spied Steve, and the man's face lit up and he waved. Jack lifted his finger. "Be right back."

Teresa pointed to the door. "She just left. You should be able to catch her."

He smiled. The awkwardness between them had dissipated when she and one of the single male volunteers had started to talk on a regular basis. "Thanks."

Rain gushed from the sky with the fervency it had the night before. He looked to the parking lot and spied Pamela beside her car, her eyes closed and her face lifted to the heavens. He raced to her and grabbed her arm. "Pamela."

She looked at him. Rain streamed down her nose and cheeks. "Jack, I've got to go. I can't do this."

"Please talk to me." He pulled on her arm, and to his surprise, she allowed him to guide her to an awning beside the shelter. "It wasn't my bottle."

She narrowed her gaze, and he opened his arms. "Look at me. I'm not hungover. I'm dirty. I'm tired. But I haven't been drinking. It was almost midnight when I got back. I went to the shelter and crashed on the couch. I slept harder than I expected."

She crossed her arms and looked away from him. He yanked the note out of his pocket. "Look. This was under the bottle. One of the volunteers had put it there to show me he'd caught one of the guys with alcohol. It's not allowed. The bottle was just proof."

Pamela took the note from his hand and read it. Her

shoulders slumped, and her lower lip quivered. "Why didn't you call us while you were gone?"

He patted his jean pockets, then his coat pockets. He pulled his phone out of the inside of his coat. "Phone got busted on the bus on the way there. I didn't have your number memorized, so I couldn't call. But I had left a message before I boarded the bus."

She frowned. "Emmy accidentally deleted it."

She didn't say anything else, and Jack waited. If he'd heard her correctly about getting back together, he wanted to give her time to digest the information. She'd always been a thinker, almost to the point of driving him crazy.

To his surprise, she reached out and took his hand in hers. "Owen told me about your mom. I'm really sorry."

Jack bit his bottom lip. "Yeah, she's battled MS for years, but we never expected her to die from a heart attack. And so young. Barely fifty."

"How's your dad and your sister and brother?"

"Hurting. But I'm praying God will use this to draw them to Himself." His voice caught. "I couldn't believe how big Kari and Todd have gotten. I wish I could see them more often. Be the big brother they need."

Pamela lifted her hand and touched his cheek. He closed his eyes and leaned into her touch. "I love you so much, Pammer."

"I know you do." She stepped closer and wrapped her arms around his waist. "I'm scared, Jack."

He wrapped his arms around her shoulders and held her against him. With his lips against her hair, he said, "You have every right to be."

"I loved you so much. Would have done anything for

you. But there were times I was afraid of you. Afraid you'd hurt me or Emma."

Jack's stomach turned, and he squeezed his eyes closed as he remembered the woman and her two girls at the shelter in Texas. "Praise God I didn't."

"I was embarrassed when you didn't help Dad and my brothers on the farm. Angry when you didn't help me with the house or Emma."

He cupped her chin and lifted her gaze to his. "All those things were inexcusable, and you have every right not to trust me again. But God has changed me."

Pamela's gaze softened. "He's changed me, too. He's given me grace despite my anger and bitterness the last few years. He's allowed me to raise two beautiful girls and go back to school, something I always wanted to do." She lifted her hands until her fingers traced through his hair. "And even though I'm scared out of my wits, he's brought you back to me."

Jack's heartbeat quickened as disbelief, excitement and joy racing through him. He lowered his head and captured her lips against his. There was no fear as she returned the kiss, and his stomach churned and his knees weakened. Pulling her tighter, he grabbed her head and kissed her forehead, her cheeks, her nose, her chin, her lips again. He didn't want to let her go. "By God's grace, I'll be good to you."

"You'd better be."

She pulled away from him, and he realized her skin had paled and her bottom lip quivered. "You're freezing."

"Just a little bit."

"Let's get you inside."

She shook her head. "No. I'll go home, take a hot shower and put on some dry clothes."

Standing on tiptoes, she cupped her hand around his neck and kissed him again. "I love you, Jack."

Jack's heart beat against his chest as she raced back to the car. His prayers had been answered. And God had said yes.

At home, Pamela touched her fingers to her lips. She could still feel Jack's kisses and found she yearned for more. Closing her eyes, she needed to keep her mind focused on what was most pressing. Before she and Jack could pursue a relationship with each other again, she'd need to talk with the girls. It had been the three of them all their lives. Adding a guy to the mix would definitely change things.

She chuckled when she remembered shaving cream and dull razors and woodsy-scented soap crowding her products in the shower. For some reason, Jack always dropped his dirty clothes beside the clothes hamper. Not in the hamper. Beside it. Something she never understood. And the toothpaste. He never put the cap back on. Constantly left the cabinets open. A zillion little things that had driven her crazy.

And she couldn't wait to battle each of them again.

After a hot shower, she dressed, blow-dried her hair, and walked to her parents' house. The girls and their grandpa sat at the kitchen table, icing sugar cookies. Her mom placed dishes in the dishwasher. "So, did you see Jack?"

Her mother acted uninterested, but Pamela knew better. Her parents were every bit as concerned as she.

"I did."

"Why hasn't he called us?" asked Emma.

Pamela wished she could wipe the concern from her older daughter's features. The girl worried far too much. Pamela hoped that would change in the coming months. She petted Emma's long hair. "Remember I told you his mother passed away."

Emmy licked her plastic knife. "Yeah. Our grandma that we haven't met."

Pamela scrunched her nose. She hated the disconnected tone in Emmy's voice. "Yes. Well, he dropped his phone on the bus and busted it, so he couldn't call us."

Emma looked relieved as she leaned back in her chair. Emmy continued to lick the knife. She'd never been concerned. How Pamela wished the girls could share just a bit of the other's personality.

Pamela continued. "My guess is we'll see him later today."

"Yay," squealed Emmy.

"How was the funeral?" asked her dad.

"He said it was hard and that his siblings have grown a lot. He hopes to see them again soon." She tapped Emmy on the nose. "He wants you two to meet them, as well."

Emmy lifted her eyebrows. "Okay by me."

Emma shrugged, then focused on the cookie she was decorating.

"What do you think about that?" Tammie asked.

"I think it would be good." Pamela picked up the dishcloth on the table and twisted it. "Girls, I'd like to talk with you." She looked at her parents. "It's okay if you stay."

They nodded, and her mom pulled up a chair and sat beside her dad. Worry was etched on her mother's brow, and Pamela almost laughed out loud. She knew where she and Emma got that characteristic.

She took one of each girl's hands in hers. "What would you think about me and your dad getting back together?"

Emmy pulled her hand away and clapped. "Yay! I always wanted a mommy and a daddy like Stephanie. She says her daddy keeps the monsters out from under the bed." She leaned closer and pursed her lips. "Course, we know there's no such thing as monsters."

Emma stared at the cookie on the table. She pulled her hand away, then set down the knife and started to get up. Pamela reached for her again. "Where are you going, Emma?"

She dropped both hands at her sides, and her face reddened as she yelled, "What if he leaves again?"

She ran out of the room and up the stairs. Emmy clicked her tongue. "Somebody needs to take a chill pill."

Pamela rolled her eyes at Emmy. She looked at her parents. "I'll be right back."

Her dad squeezed her hand. "We're happy for you, and Emma will be okay."

As she walked up the stairs, she heard Emmy's words. "My daddy's back for good. He…"

Her daughter's voice faded as Pamela walked to the back bedroom, where she knew Emma would be. She opened the door and saw Emma curled up in the oversize yellow wingback chair, her arms wrapped around her legs and her chin resting on her knees. She stared out the window. The rain had finally stopped, and the sun peeked through the clouds every few minutes.

Pamela sat on the edge of the bed. "You wanna talk about it?"

Emma turned and looked at Pamela. "I like that it's just you and me and Emmy."

"What do you think about your dad?"

Emma shrugged. "He's okay." She rolled her eyes. "Emmy likes him good enough for both of us."

Pamela grinned. "I think you're right."

"Uncle Ben said that he was no good and should go back where he came from."

Pamela bit her bottom lip. She wished Ben would have kept his thoughts to himself. She understood he was concerned about Jack coming back into their lives, but not once had he given Jack the chance to show him that he'd changed. "What do you think about your dad? Is he no good?"

Emma shook her head.

"Has he been taking care of us since he came back to Bloom Hollow?"

Emma shrugged. "He didn't call the last two days."

"His phone was broken."

She dropped her chin back onto her knees. "I know."

"I've been praying about this, Emma." She paused. How much should she tell her daughter? The girl was only nine. *God, guide me.* "And I've been scared."

Emma looked up, her gaze searching Pamela's for truth and confirmation. "I was really sad when your dad left. And I have been scared." She clasped her hands. "But I've decided that I have to trust your dad to God."

"But what if—"

Pamela walked to her daughter and placed her hand on her shoulder. "Life is going to be full of what-ifs. All we can do is trust God with what He's asking us to do. Your dad loves us, and—"

"Do you love him, Mom?"

Pamela nodded, and her heart swelled with peace. "I do."

Emma looked back out the window. "I guess I do, too."

Pamela lifted her daughter's chin and looked her in the eye. "It's going to be okay. God's got it."

Chapter 19

The past few days had been bliss for Jack. He'd shared with Pastor Mark about the reconciliation, and he had allowed Jack every opportunity to spend time with Pamela and the girls. Christmas was only days away, and he could hardly wait to enjoy the holiday with his daughters for the first time.

"Where are we going, Dad?" asked Emma from the backseat of the car.

"I thought we'd visit the shelter where I work. We've received a bunch of clothes that we need to sort, and I thought you girls could help."

"Cool," said Emmy.

Emma wrinkled her nose, and Jack laughed. "Doesn't sound fun to you, Emma?"

She shook her head. "Not really."

Pamela reached over and grabbed his hand. "It will be great."

They reached the shelter and, since dinner wasn't for a few hours, he took them on a tour. The girls' eyes widened when they saw the dining area. Emma pointed to the walls. "There are scriptures all over the place."

"Yep," said Jack.

"I think it's cool." She pointed to the door leading to the kitchen. "What's in there?"

He took them into the room.

"You have a serving line like at school," said Emmy.

"We do," said Jack.

Emma pointed to appliances. "Does the school have that many stoves and refrigerators?"

Pamela laughed. "I don't know."

He showed them his office, and Emmy hopped on his rolling chair and spun around several times. Finally, they made it to the back room. A pile of clothes nearly as tall as him sat in the corner.

The girls' eyes widened. "Whoa," they said together.

Pamela lifted her eyebrows. "That is quite a stack, Jack." She covered her mouth and giggled at the rhyme, and Jack planted a quick kiss on her nose.

He rolled up his sleeves. "Okay. This is how we'll separate them. A pile for boys' clothes. Another for girls'. A third for women. A fourth for men. And the last—" he picked up a ragged shirt that had multiple holes "—will be for clothes that aren't good enough to be given away."

Pamela clapped her hands. "Got it."

Emmy dug in, chattering as she separated items into the different piles. Every once in a while, she'd ooh over a shirt she liked or wrinkle her nose at something she found to be "gross."

Emma seemed a bit hesitant, so Jack stayed close. He talked to her about Christmas and the present they'd bought Pamela. Soon, she settled in and smiled at Emmy's exclamations over the apparel.

The dinner crew arrived to prepare the meal, and Jack left his family for a few minutes to make sure everything was ready in the kitchen. When he returned, the girls had finished separating and even put the unusable clothes in trash bags. He high-fived each of them. "Great job! I think you've earned some chicken nuggets tonight."

Emmy pumped her fist. "Yes!"

"I thought we might eat here."

The girls' jaws dropped at Pamela's suggestion. Jack lifted his eyebrows, every bit as surprised as them.

"Are you kidding?" said Emma.

Pamela placed her hand on their older daughter's back. "I'm not." She shrugged her right shoulder. "We'll get to see what your dad does."

Jack rubbed his hands together. "That sounds great." He opened his palms. "We could go for ice cream afterward."

Emmy twisted her hips. "Oh, all right."

"There is one more thing I'd like to do," said Jack.

Emma smacked her hand against her forehead. "Please don't tell me we have to sort food."

Jack and Pamela laughed, and he said, "No. I'd like you to meet my dad and sister and brother."

The girls frowned, and Emmy raised her palms upward. "How?"

"Have you heard of Skype?" said Pamela.

They walked back into his office and he turned on the computer. He pulled his phone out of his pocket and texted Kari to tell them to get ready.

Emma pointed to the screen. "Isn't that like through the computer?"

Jack typed in his account number and password. "It is. And they're already waiting to meet you both."

"They are?" said Emmy.

Kari's face popped up on the screen. She motioned beside her. "Guys, come here. They're on."

Jack waved at the screen. "Hey, Kari. They're ready."

Both girls squeezed their faces close to the screen. At first, they kept leaning forward and backward, looking at themselves in the box at the top of the screen. Soon Todd had them laughing at the ridiculous faces he was making. Looking at the clock on the screen, Jack knew dinner had started several minutes ago. "I'm sorry, everyone, but we're going to have to get off now."

The girls whined, and Kari pouted through the screen. They said goodbye and promised to call again soon; then he led the family into the dining hall. Emma grabbed his hand when they saw some of the homeless people taking trays to various tables. Jack peeked at the door to be sure someone was greeting their guests and checking bags. Teresa was there, and he let out a sigh of relief.

He guided them through the serving line. They didn't pay any attention to the food or the volunteers, even though the people oohed and aahed over the girls. Both of them stared at the homeless, and he wished he could venture through their minds to know what they were thinking.

They set the food on an open table and Steve walked up behind the girls. "What have we here?"

The girls jumped, and Emmy placed her hand on her chest. Emma grabbed Jack's hand and squeezed, and Emmy moved closer to Pamela. Jack smiled at Steve. "These are my girls. Emma and Emmy."

Steve bent down and tapped Emmy on the nose. "Well, aren't you just the cutest little girls I've ever seen."

Emmy leaned closer to Pamela.

He turned and looked at Emma. "Do you mind if I sit with you?"

Jack swallowed. Under normal circumstances he'd never deny Steve the opportunity to sit with him for dinner. But this was the girls' first trip to the shelter, and even though they were safe with him by their sides, he knew they didn't feel comfortable.

To his surprise, Emma nodded and sat down in a seat. She pointed to the place beside her. "You can sit here."

Jack looked at Pamela, and she grinned and shrugged. They all sat and started to eat fried chicken, mashed potatoes and peas. Steve talked to the girls about his life as a boy, and soon the girls were giggling at his tales of leaving lizards in the teacher's desk and snakes in her closet. Jack hoped those things weren't true, but he couldn't be sure as mischievous as he'd discovered Steve to be.

When dinner ended, Steve tugged at Emma's hair. "You girls will have to come back on Thursday. Hamburger night." He rubbed his belly. "My favorite night of the week."

After making sure the dinner crew had all the cleanup under way for the night, Jack and his family walked to the car. He'd driven less than five minutes before Emmy had fallen asleep in the back.

"Dad," Emma said.

"Yes, honey?"

"Let's skip ice cream and go home. I think we've had enough excitement for one night."

"Sounds good to me." Jack peeked at Pamela, and she covered her mouth to keep from laughing. Out of the mouths of babes.

Pamela heard a car pull into the driveway. She knew it was Ben. She excused herself from finishing the preparations for their Christmas Eve dinner and rushed outside. Dad, Kirk and Jack all sat in the living area chatting about which teams would end up in the Super Bowl while she, Mom, Callie and the girls worked peaceably in the kitchen. The last thing she wanted was for Ben to come in the house and throw a fit about Jack.

Ben opened the car door and lifted his hand to her. "I already told you on the phone. I'm not gonna say anything to your *precious* husband."

Pamela blew out a breath and hugged her overgrown little brother. "Merry Christmas, Ben."

He huffed. "Sure. Whatever."

She worried about him. He'd had to take a year longer than he expected to finish school, and her dad had mentioned some credit card debt. Which she didn't understand since he had a free ride and a part-time job. At least, they thought he had a job.

Whatever was going on, the bitterness and anger he showed tore at her heartstrings. She understood the feelings all too well and knew they would only bring him sadness.

He opened the back door of the car and grabbed a few presents. She took some out, as well. "I know we talked on the phone, but I just wanted to say that Jack has changed. I want you to give him a chance."

"Listen, Pamela. I said I'd be nice to him for the girls, but you can't make me like him."

He shut the door with his hip and stalked toward the door. Pamela followed him. The girls squealed when they saw him, and he tickled both of them. When the men came into the kitchen, he was nice as he promised, saying hello to Jack, but it was obvious he didn't want to.

Kirk clapped his hands. "Now that we're all here. Callie and I have a present we'd like to give Mom and Dad before we get started on dinner and gifts and such."

Callie bit her bottom lip and grinned as she took a rectangular box out of the bag that hung on the back of one of the chairs. "Here you go."

Mom placed her hand on her chest. "What is it?"

"I think it'll say if they're having boys or girls," said Dad.

"Really," said Mom. "But I thought you weren't going to find out."

"Open it, Grandma." Emmy jumped in front of her.

"Boys," said Dad.

Pamela shook her head. "Nope. Girls."

Ben chuckled. "I'd love to see Kirk end up with two girls at one time."

"Two girls is okay," whined Emma.

"Yes, they are," said Jack.

Callie wrapped her arms around Kirk's waist and nestled her nose against his chest. In the past, the show of affection would have made Pamela jealous. She grabbed Jack's hand. Now she just felt thankful that God had blessed her with love again.

Kirk blew out a breath. "We never said it was gonna tell you what we're having."

Dad winked. "But I'm sure that's what it is."

Emmy dropped her hands at her sides. "Just open it already, Grandma."

Pamela grinned as her mother tore open the paper. She lifted off the top and pulled out a picture frame. She cackled as she read the front.

"Well, what's it say?" Mike asked.

Her mom turned it around. On the left side was a sonogram picture of one of the twins with its hand in the air. Beneath the picture were the words *I'm a boy.* On the right side was a picture of the other twin with the words *So am I* beneath it.

The family cheered, and Kirk pumped the air with his fist. "Got my boys just like I said."

Emmy punched Kirk's arm. "What's wrong with girls?"

He wrapped his arm around her neck and scratched the top of her head with his knuckles. "Not a thing wrong with girls, except that y'all have been outnumbering us boys for too long."

Jack squeezed Pamela's hand, leaned close and whispered, "Maybe that will be us again."

She huffed. "Not for a while."

Even though they'd need time to rebuild their relationship and grow as a family, in the depths of her heart she relished the idea of maybe one day having another baby with Jack. But not for a while.

Chapter 20

Jack took another swig of coffee as Emma and Emmy opened the last of their presents. Pamela had called him at five o'clock to tell him the girls had awakened and were ready for presents. He hadn't hesitated to jump in the car and drive to the cabin, but he couldn't wait until he and Pamela and the girls lived under one roof.

He tapped the front pocket of his flannel shirt to check once again that he hadn't forgotten Pamela's gift. He'd noticed last night that she wore her engagement and wedding rings again. The one in his pocket would match the set nicely.

He rubbed his thumb against his band. He'd hocked it for alcohol several years ago, but soon after accepting Christ and sobering up, he'd gone back to the pawn shop, and, to his surprise, the ring had still been there.

"Mom, can we ride our bikes out by the orchard?" asked Emmy.

Emma nodded. "Yeah. We'll stay on the dirt path close to the house."

"I don't know, girls." She looked at Jack. "What time do we need to leave for the shelter?"

He looked at his phone and winked at the girls. "We have a few hours. I think they have time."

"Okay, but it's cold outside." Pamela stood up and grabbed their coats out of the closet. Jack grinned as she fussed over the girls; zipping them up all the way and making sure they had gloves. It felt good to be with his family on Christmas, to watch the joy in his girls' eyes as they opened presents, to receive kisses as thanks.

The girls walked their bikes outside, and Pamela opened the curtains. They could see the girls riding on the path. Pamela sat beside him on the couch. "I have a present for you."

He sniffed. "Apple crisps?"

She swatted his arm. "Well, those were supposed to be a surprise."

He kissed the tip of her nose. "You don't think I can smell your apple crisps the moment I walk through the door?"

She pushed him away, then leaned over the arm of the couch and lifted up a present. "It isn't much, but the girls and I thought you might like it."

Jack tore off the paper and opened the box. He pulled out a framed portrait of all three of them.

She shrugged. "We figured you might want to put it on your desk at work."

Jack held it to his chest. "I've wanted a picture of the three of you for a long time." He swallowed the knot in his throat. "I have something for you, too."

"Jack," she sighed. "You already bought me too much. Shoes. A sweater. A gift card to get my hair cut. A…"

Jack knelt down on one knee.

She giggled, and her cheeks flushed. "Jack, we're already married."

He pulled the ring out of his front shirt pocket. "We haven't been really married in over eight years. We will celebrate our tenth wedding anniversary this summer, but I didn't honor those vows the way a husband should."

She frowned. "But you said—"

"I loved you, and I was faithful to you, but I wasn't here when you needed me. Pammer, I want to renew those vows before God and our families. This ring was the first purchase I made after accepting Christ and sobering up."

Pamela gasped. "You've had this for three years?"

Jack nodded, thinking of the many times he'd looked at the ring and reminded himself that he would one day be able to put it on her finger. "I've asked your dad—"

Pamela placed her hand on her chest. "You asked my dad?"

Jack chuckled at all her questions. "Yes, I asked your dad." He moved closer to her and cupped his hand against her cheek. "I don't want to live apart from you anymore. I love you, and I want you to be my wife in every way."

Pamela twisted her mouth. "I'm not sure I'm ready to deal with all your clothes lying next to the hamper."

He narrowed his gaze. "I'll pick them up. If I remember right, someone liked to shave her armpits and legs with my razor."

Pamela cocked her head and wrinkled her nose. "Well, you know if someone leaves them all crowded up in the shower, then someone else might not have a choice."

Jack dipped his chin and glared at her. "Pammer."

She scooted forward on the couch and wrapped both hands around his neck. She kissed his lips in one swift motion. "I'd love to renew our vows."

He grabbed her waist and pulled her into his lap. Tracing his fingers through her hair, he pressed his lips against hers. Her fingernails scratched his neck, and shivers raced down his spine. He growled. "I'm thinking we're going to have to renew those vows soon. Valentine's Day?"

She shook her head. "No."

His chest caved. "Then when?"

"New Year's."

He pulled back. "Seven days?"

"Too soon?"

He kissed her again. "Not at all. New Year's, it is."

Pamela chuckled when she saw her parents' living room. The Christmas tree still stood in the corner, but all the furnishings were gone. Only ten folding chairs decorated with white tulle bows and red ribbon sat in front of the fireplace.

The ceremony would be anything but traditional, since she and her groom were already married, and yet butterflies still fluttered in her belly, and, once again, she looked forward to her wedding night. Eight years was a long time.

Emmy ran into the room. She looked lovely in the short-sleeved red velvet dress with the floral soutache design beneath the waist. A thin sequined ribbon wrapped around her tiny stomach, adding a bit of bling that Emmy loved, but not so much that Emma would hate it. "My hair messed up."

Pamela pulled a bobby pin out of Emmy's hair and then pushed it in again. The partial updo was too old a style for her eight- and nine-year-old girls, but Kari had done such a good job, and the girls adored the attention from their teenage aunt.

"Go get your sister. Let me see how pretty she looks, as well." She swatted Emmy's behind, and Emmy raced into the other room.

Emma walked into the living room, tugging Jack's dad by the hand. He clasped his hands and rubbed them together. "You look beautiful, Pamela."

Pamela's cheeks warmed. She felt beautiful. More so than she had in years. She'd spent over an hour curling her hair; then she'd clipped a rhinestone barrette in the back, allowing the curls to spill down her left shoulder.

She hadn't wanted to wear white. Felt it would be silly, but Jack had talked her into it. He'd said it was a clean start for them. Pure. When she'd tried on the floor-length white satin gown, she'd known he was right. Aside from the short rhinestone sleeves that attached to a sweetheart neckline, the dress was simple and elegant and gorgeous.

"Thank you, Henry."

She'd worried her first meeting with Jack's dad would be awkward, but Henry had been very kind and apologetic that they hadn't kept in touch. He'd played every game the girls owned multiple times in the past few days, and she knew she would be seeing a lot of Jack's family from now on.

Kari hustled into the room, and Pamela marveled again at how much she'd grown and how lovely she looked. There was no mistaking that she, Todd and Jack were siblings. Kari grabbed Pamela's hand and pulled her into the kitchen. "Get in here with me. You should be the last one everybody sees."

Pamela laughed. "This isn't a traditional wedding, you know."

"But still."

A whistle sounded from behind her. Pamela turned and saw Kirk and Callie standing in the back door. Kirk grabbed her in a hug. "Who knew my sister was such a looker?"

Pamela swatted his shoulder and took in his khakis and red button-down shirt. "Who knew my brother could clean up?"

Callie blew out a breath and shook her head. "It took a lot of work."

Kirk grabbed her and nuzzled his nose into her neck. Callie squealed and punched his arm. "Kirk, you'll make me wet myself."

Pamela burst out laughing, and Kari's jaw dropped. Callie tapped Kari's arm, then pointed at her belly. "I'm carrying twins."

Pamela pointed to the living area. "You two better have a seat before Mom catches you acting so silly."

Todd walked into the kitchen, pulling at his dark blue necktie. "Kari, I can't figure this thing out."

His sister retied the knot and straightened his collar. "You look handsome, little brother."

Pamela nodded her agreement.

"What about this little brother?"

Pamela turned and saw Ben towering in the back door. Out of the corner of her eye, she saw Kari's cheeks darken, and Pamela bit back a chuckle. She couldn't deny he was a good-looking guy. She adjusted Ben's tie. "You look mighty handsome, as well."

"And you look beautiful."

"Thanks, Ben."

He nodded to Kari and walked past her. Pamela knew he didn't agree with the reconciliation, but he was here, and that was all that mattered.

Her mom and dad walked into the kitchen. Her dad kissed the side of her head. "Now don't you look lovely?"

Mom pursed her lips. "Pamela, what are you doing down here? Has Jack seen you?"

"Thanks, Dad." She grinned at her mother. "Mom, you know Jack and I are already technically married."

"I know, but you haven't technically lived together in eight years. This is special. I know Jack wants—"

She took her mom's hand. "It is special. Very special. And the living room is amazing."

Her mom let out a long breath and smiled. She touched Pamela's cheek, and her eyes brimmed with tears. "I'm so happy for you."

"Me, too."

Tammie grabbed a paper towel off the counter and dabbed her eyes. She took Kari's hand. "Why don't you and I find ourselves a seat?" She turned to Pamela's dad. "You are walking her in, right?"

"Of course."

Pamela huffed. "I don't think that's necessary."

Her dad shrugged. "Jack asked."

She rolled her eyes. "Okay." She wrapped her arm around her dad's and started toward the door.

"We have to wait for the music."

"There's music?"

He nodded. Within moments a country song spieled

through the room, proclaiming love that hadn't ended. The woman sang that her man was still the one she loved. The words fit their relationship perfectly. Despite all that had happened, she loved Jack with every ounce of her being, and, by God's grace, he would be the one for the rest of her life.

She walked through the door and spied Jack beside Pastor Mark in front of the fireplace. Jack's eyes lit up and a smile spread across his face. The walk took only a moment, but she believed she would never make it to his arms. She couldn't take her eyes off him as they vowed their love once again, a promise before God and their families.

When Pastor Mark announced them as renewed husband and wife, Pamela took her husband's cheeks in her hands and kissed his lips.

Emmy squealed. "Daddy's gonna live with us."

Emma added, "Yep. We're a family."

Pamela offered a prayer of thanksgiving to God. They were a family. A family reunited.

* * * * *

REQUEST YOUR FREE BOOKS!
2 FREE WHOLESOME ROMANCE NOVELS IN LARGER PRINT
PLUS 2 FREE MYSTERY GIFTS

✿✿✿✿✿✿✿✿✿✿✿✿✿✿✿✿✿✿✿✿✿✿✿

HEARTWARMING™
🎄🎄🎄🎄🎄🎄🎄🎄🎄🎄🎄🎄🎄🎄🎄🎄🎄

Wholesome, tender romances

YES! Please send me 2 FREE Harlequin® Heartwarming Larger-Print novels and my 2 FREE mystery gifts (gifts worth about $10). After receiving them, if I don't wish to receive any more books, I can return the shipping statement marked "cancel." If I don't cancel, I will receive 4 brand-new larger-print novels every month and be billed just $4.99 per book in the U.S. or $5.74 per book in Canada. That's a savings of at least 23% off the cover price. It's quite a bargain! Shipping and handling is just 50¢ per book in the U.S. and 75¢ per book in Canada.* I understand that accepting the 2 free books and gifts places me under no obligation to buy anything. I can always return a shipment and cancel at any time. Even if I never buy another book, the two free books and gifts are mine to keep forever.

161/361 IDN F47N

Name _____ (PLEASE PRINT)

Address _____ Apt. #

City _____ State/Prov. _____ Zip/Postal Code

Signature (if under 18, a parent or guardian must sign)

Mail to the **Harlequin® Reader Service:**
IN U.S.A.: P.O. Box 1867, Buffalo, NY 14240-1867
IN CANADA: P.O. Box 609, Fort Erie, Ontario L2A 5X3

* Terms and prices subject to change without notice. Prices do not include applicable taxes. Sales tax applicable in N.Y. Canadian residents will be charged applicable taxes. Offer not valid in Quebec. This offer is limited to one order per household. Not valid for current subscribers to Harlequin Heartwarming larger-print books. All orders subject to credit approval. Credit or debit balances in a customer's account(s) may be offset by any other outstanding balance owed by or to the customer. Please allow 4 to 6 weeks for delivery. Offer available while quantities last.

Your Privacy—The Harlequin® Reader Service is committed to protecting your privacy. Our Privacy Policy is available online at www.ReaderService.com or upon request from the Harlequin Reader Service.

We make a portion of our mailing list available to reputable third parties that offer products we believe may interest you. If you prefer that we not exchange your name with third parties, or if you wish to clarify or modify your communication preferences, please visit us at www.ReaderService.com/consumerchoice or write to us at Harlequin Reader Service Preference Service, P.O. Box 9062, Buffalo, NY 14269. Include your complete name and address.

HWDIR13R

REQUEST YOUR FREE BOOKS!

2 FREE INSPIRATIONAL NOVELS
PLUS 2
FREE
MYSTERY GIFTS

Love Inspired.
HISTORICAL
INSPIRATIONAL HISTORICAL ROMANCE

YES! Please send me 2 FREE Love Inspired® Historical novels and my 2 FREE mystery gifts (gifts are worth about $10). After receiving them, if I don't wish to receive any more books, I can return the shipping statement marked "cancel." If I don't cancel, I will receive 4 brand-new novels every month and be billed just $4.74 per book in the U.S. or $5.24 per book in Canada. That's a savings of at least 21% off the cover price. It's quite a bargain! Shipping and handling is just 50¢ per book in the U.S. and 75¢ per book in Canada.* I understand that accepting the 2 free books and gifts places me under no obligation to buy anything. I can always return a shipment and cancel at any time. Even if I never buy another book, the two free books and gifts are mine to keep forever.

102/302 IDN F5CY

Name	(PLEASE PRINT)
Address	Apt. #
City	State/Prov.	Zip/Postal Code

Signature (if under 18, a parent or guardian must sign)

Mail to the Harlequin® Reader Service:
IN U.S.A.: P.O. Box 1867, Buffalo, NY 14240-1867
IN CANADA: P.O. Box 609, Fort Erie, Ontario L2A 5X3

Want to try two free books from another series?
Call 1-800-873-8635 or visit www.ReaderService.com.

* Terms and prices subject to change without notice. Prices do not include applicable taxes. Sales tax applicable in N.Y. Canadian residents will be charged applicable taxes. Offer not valid in Quebec. This offer is limited to one order per household. Not valid for current subscribers to Love Inspired Historical books. All orders subject to credit approval. Credit or debit balances in a customer's account(s) may be offset by any other outstanding balance owed by or to the customer. Please allow 4 to 6 weeks for delivery. Offer available while quantities last.

Your Privacy—The Harlequin® Reader Service is committed to protecting your privacy. Our Privacy Policy is available online at www.ReaderService.com or upon request from the Harlequin Reader Service.

We make a portion of our mailing list available to reputable third parties that offer products we believe may interest you. If you prefer that we not exchange your name with third parties, or if you wish to clarify or modify your communication preferences, please visit us at www.ReaderService.com/consumerchoice or write to us at Harlequin Reader Service Preference Service, P.O. Box 9062, Buffalo, NY 14269. Include your complete name and address.

LIHDIR13R

REQUEST YOUR FREE BOOKS!

2 FREE INSPIRATIONAL NOVELS
PLUS 2
FREE
MYSTERY GIFTS

Love Inspired

YES! Please send me 2 FREE Love Inspired® novels and my 2 FREE mystery gifts (gifts are worth about $10). After receiving them, if I don't wish to receive any more books, I can return the shipping statement marked "cancel." If I don't cancel, I will receive 6 brand-new novels every month and be billed just $4.74 per book in the U.S. or $5.24 per book in Canada. That's a savings of at least 21% off the cover price. It's quite a bargain! Shipping and handling is just 50¢ per book in the U.S. and 75¢ per book in Canada.* I understand that accepting the 2 free books and gifts places me under no obligation to buy anything. I can always return a shipment and cancel at any time. Even if I never buy another book, the two free books and gifts are mine to keep forever.

105/305 IDN F49N

Name _____ (PLEASE PRINT)

Address _____ Apt. #

City _____ State/Prov. _____ Zip/Postal Code

Signature (if under 18, a parent or guardian must sign)

Mail to the **Harlequin® Reader Service:**
IN U.S.A.: P.O. Box 1867, Buffalo, NY 14240-1867
IN CANADA: P.O. Box 609, Fort Erie, Ontario L2A 5X3

**Are you a subscriber to Love Inspired books
and want to receive the larger-print edition?
Call 1-800-873-8635 or visit www.ReaderService.com.**

* Terms and prices subject to change without notice. Prices do not include applicable taxes. Sales tax applicable in N.Y. Canadian residents will be charged applicable taxes. Offer not valid in Quebec. This offer is limited to one order per household. Not valid for current subscribers to Love Inspired books. All orders subject to credit approval. Credit or debit balances in a customer's account(s) may be offset by any other outstanding balance owed by or to the customer. Please allow 4 to 6 weeks for delivery. Offer available while quantities last.

Your Privacy—The Harlequin® Reader Service is committed to protecting your privacy. Our Privacy Policy is available online at www.ReaderService.com or upon request from the Harlequin Reader Service.
We make a portion of our mailing list available to reputable third parties that offer products we believe may interest you. If you prefer that we not exchange your name with third parties, or if you wish to clarify or modify your communication preferences, please visit us at www.ReaderService.com/consumerchoice or write to us at Harlequin Reader Service Preference Service, P.O. Box 9062, Buffalo, NY 14269. Include your complete name and address.

LIDIR13R

Reader Service.com

Manage your account online!

- Review your order history
- Manage your payments
- Update your address

*We've designed
the Harlequin® Reader Service
website just for you.*

Enjoy all the features!

- Reader excerpts from any series
- Respond to mailings and
  special monthly offers
- Discover new series available to you
- Browse the Bonus Bucks catalog
- Share your feedback

Visit us at:

ReaderService.com